We laughed together and it was like being back at the Hotel de Paris, when we'd chatted for hours and known each other better in that time than some people do in a lifetime.

The music was smoochy. He drew me close so that my head rested on his shoulder, and he dropped his own head, turning it slightly in to my neck so that his lips brushed my skin.

It was physically exciting, and added to my frustration that I couldn't have him. But it was also strangely cosy. The warmth that swept me was contentment. I could gladly nestle against him like this forever.

Only it wasn't going to be forever. Another week, perhaps less. Already I felt more in tune with him than was wise, but I knew I couldn't be wise. Not with Jack. There was all the rest of my life for wisdom.

Lucy Gordon cut her writing teeth on magazine journalism, interviewing many of the world's most interesting men, including Warren Beatty, Richard Chamberlain, Roger Moore, Sir Alec Guinness and Sir John Gielgud. She also camped out with lions in Africa, and had many other unusual experiences which have often provided the background for her books. She is married to a Venetian, whom she met while on holiday in Venice. They got engaged within two days.

Two of her books have won the Romance Writers of America RITA® award—*Song of the Lorelei* and *His Brother's Child* in the Best Traditional Romance category.

You can visit her Web site at www.lucy-gordon.com

THE MONTE CARLO PROPOSAL

Lucy Gordon

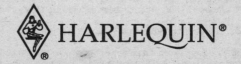

HARLEQUIN®

TORONTO • NEW YORK • LONDON
AMSTERDAM • PARIS • SYDNEY • HAMBURG
STOCKHOLM • ATHENS • TOKYO • MILAN • MADRID
PRAGUE • WARSAW • BUDAPEST • AUCKLAND

ISBN 0-373-18177-9

THE MONTE CARLO PROPOSAL

First North American Publication 2005.

www.eHarlequin.com

Printed in U.S.A.

CHAPTER ONE

Della's Story

IT WAS a great dress. No argument. Silver and slinky, low-cut in the front and high-slit at the side. It had some magic quality that made my hips and bust look bigger and my waist look smaller, and it fitted so closely that you just knew I was wearing nothing underneath. And I mean nothing. That dress was cool, sexy, provocative, sensational.

At any other time I'd have loved it. But not now. Not now I knew why that slimeball Hugh Vanner had been so eager to get it on me. It was because he wanted one, or more, of his equally slimy 'business associates' to get it off me.

And since it was a moot question whether they were more disgusting or he was—no way!

At this point a woman with her head screwed on would have got out—fast. But that's not easy when you're on a yacht. Even if it is moored in the harbour at Monte Carlo.

I'd been hired in London as a waitress, and I suppose it was naïve of me to think that 'waitress' meant waitress. But I was in a tight hole financially.

Usually I demonstrated goods in department stores, but one job had just finished and another had just fallen through. I couldn't afford to go even a week without work, and the money being offered for this trip was good. So I crossed my fingers and hoped.

Fatal mistake.

Never cross your fingers. It makes it so hard to fight the creeps off.

I joined the yacht at Southampton. It was called *The Silverado*, and it wasn't what most people would mean by yacht, with sails and things. This was a rich man's version, over two hundred feet long, with thirteen staterooms, a bar, a swimming pool, a dining room that could seat twenty, and not a sail in sight. That kind of yacht.

My nose was twitching before I'd been on board for five minutes. The place shrieked too much of the wrong sort of money in the hands of the wrong sort of people who'd acquired it by the wrong sort of means.

Don't get me wrong. I like money. But, for reasons I can't go into now, I'm nervous about where it comes from. I've known life when anything I wanted could be served up on a plate, and life when I didn't know where my next penny was coming from.

I was in one of those times now, so I stayed on board and got stuck into the job.

No. Scratch that last phrase. I stayed on board and worked hard. Better.

I didn't meet Vanner until several hours later, and the whole grubby, sweaty mess of him came as a nasty surprise.

'You'll do,' he grunted, looking me up and down. 'I told that agency I wanted lookers. I like my guests to have a good time. Puts them in the right mood, if you know what I mean.'

I was beginning to know exactly what he meant. I was also beginning to wish I'd never come on this trip, but we were already at sea and it was too late.

'So you're Della Martin?' he demanded, breathing booze fumes over me. 'How old are you?'

'Twenty-four.'

'You look younger.'

I knew it, and it was the bane of my life. I've got a face that would be right on an eighteen-year-old, all big eyes and high cheekbones. My hair's red, and I cut it short in an attempt to make myself look more grown-up.

Fatal mistake. I end up with the look they

call *gamine*. Some women would be glad to have it. I thought it made me seem like a kid.

But Vanner loved it.

'You'd be great if only you'd smile,' he said. 'Look cheerful. Everyone on my yacht must be cheerful.'

He was always talking about 'my yacht', but it wasn't his, whatever he liked to pretend. He'd chartered it.

The trip was supposed to be a business convention, but it turned out to be Vanner cruising the Mediterranean with a gaggle of men—some with girlfriends, some alone, but none with wives.

I shared a cabin with Maggie, who was definitely a woman of the world and knew what she was there for.

'Plenty of rich pickings,' she told me on the first evening. 'Enough for both of us.'

That was true, and since rich pickings were what I needed I was probably being unreasonable in backing off. I knew Maggie thought so. But she shrugged and said, 'More for me.'

It wasn't too bad at first. There was a bit of groping, but nothing that I couldn't defuse with a laugh. I ignored the suggestive remarks, and one way or another I survived until we reached Monte Carlo.

Vanner was in a bad mood as soon as we

arrived, and I guessed it was because of the other yacht nearby. It was called *The Hawk*, and it was *The Silverado* with knobs on—at least a hundred feet longer, probably with more staterooms and a bigger swimming pool. Anyway, it made Vanner's yacht look piddling, and he didn't like it.

Mind you, he perked up when he found out who was aboard.

Jack Bullen.

Bullen was a predator, a financial genius, a bruiser who operated through the money markets instead of with his fists. But the damage was just as real to the victims.

He'd started small and become one of the richest men in the country. Even his name was useful to him. Sometimes they called him 'Jack Bullion' because of the way his money mounted up, but mostly they called him 'Bully Jack', because of his methods.

He was all over the financial pages for one master stroke or another. I can't say I normally read those pages, but I come from a family that's deeply interested in money, especially other people's. So I knew of him.

Bully Jack could afford to buy what he liked, do what he liked, and ignore what he didn't like. And few people could stand up to him.

That alone was enough to win Vanner's swooning admiration and get him grovelling.

I have to admit that the sight of Vanner grovelling was impressive. Nauseating, but impressive. He bought diamond-studded solid gold cufflinks and sent them over as a gift. They arrived back almost at once, with a brief note thanking Mr Vanner but saying Mr Bullen did not accept gifts from strange men.

I almost liked Bullen for that. But then I thought maybe I'd imagined the dead-pan humour in the note. No man so filthy rich could have made a joke so neat.

Besides, it conflicted with my image of him as a thickset thug. I'd never seen him, but there was something about his name that suggested a bone-crusher, not a wit.

Next Vanner tried a ship-to-ship phone call, with an invitation to dinner, but was informed that Mr Bullen and his guests had gone ashore and would not be returning until late.

After that Vanner's temper hit the skids. I was the first one to feel it.

'You're not pulling your weight, Della,' he snapped.

'What?' I said crossly. 'I'm doing double shifts because Maggie's never around when she's supposed to be.'

'She's involved in…other duties. Very popular girl. But you're leaving her to do it all.'

'Now, look, Mr Vanner, I'm here as a waitress.'

He gave the silent laugh that made me feel queasy.

'Of course you are, Della. Of course you are. But a very special kind of waitress. It's not enough to serve food and drink to the guests. You've got to make them feel happy.'

'I do. I smile and tell jokes, and I don't back off when they breathe fumes over me.'

His manner became ingratiating, which should have warned me.

'Of course. I know you're trying, but you're not making the best of yourself. I've had a pretty dress put in your cabin and I want you to wear it.'

I knew the worst as soon as I saw that 'pretty dress'. I should never have put it on, but we'd soon be heading back to England. Having coped for most of the trip, I thought I could manage just a bit longer.

There was one guest in particular whose piggy eyes lit up at the sight of me all silver, shimmering and half naked. His name was Rufus Telsor and he'd given me the most trouble from the start.

He'd come aboard with another man, called

Williams, whom he seemed to know well, which at first made me hope he might be gay. No such luck! They were just hunting in pairs.

I discovered that when the two of them cornered me on deck. The ensuing conversation was of the 'Come on, you know you want it really' variety, and I won't bore you with the details.

I managed to fight them off and escape with a torn dress, but I knew there was nowhere to hide on the yacht. I had to get off before they caught me again.

Going down the gangway was out of the question. Vanner was there and he would see me. Besides, go down to what? We were moored out in deep water. I'd need a boat to get to shore, and there was no way I'd be able to get one.

From the stern of the ship I had a view of him, leaning on the rail, brandy balloon in hand. Even from this distance I could see that he was red-faced and slipping out of control. I could expect no help from him. He was more likely to be furious that I'd fought back.

As I watched, Telsor and Williams appeared, heading for Vanner, presumably to complain about the lack of hospitality. I hadn't much time. It would have to be the water.

I hoisted the dress up, climbed over the rail, and jumped.

Luckily I'm a good swimmer, and I can hold my breath for a long time. When I finally surfaced I'd put some distance between me and *The Silverado*. But I was getting too close to *The Hawk* for comfort, so I kicked out and headed for the shore.

When I reached the quay I'd have had a problem if someone hadn't been passing and given me a hand up.

Briefly I toyed with the idea of asking him for help, but he wasn't alone. His companion was female and suspicious. One look at me was enough to make her squeal, 'Come *on*. We're going to be late.'

'Er—yes—er—'

He was trying to ogle me and avert his eyes at the same time. Looking down at myself, I understood. The water had made the silver dress almost transparent.

'Can you tell me how to find the British Consul?' I begged.

'No idea,' he said hastily. 'But you might find someone at the casino who'd know. Lots of Brits there. Head up that hill. *Coming, Gina!*'

And he was gone.

I began to climb up the slope that led to the

town. It was hard because I'd lost my shoes in the water. Plus I had to keep to the shadows, in case I got arrested for going around half naked.

I managed to make it to the casino, and slip into the gardens without attracting attention, but then I realised I had a problem.

What should I do? Walk in like this?

There was an open door, with light pouring from within. I could make out the shapes of people moving back and forth, the sound of music and laughter. It was a tempting scene, the kind where I would once have been at home.

Gamblers, people who live on the edge, high rollers: I'd always felt comfortable with them. That buzz of anticipation is something I understand. Well, in my family you have to.

But right now I was on the outside looking in, desperate, stranded, not a penny to my name, nothing but the clothes I was almost wearing.

Then something happened.

A man came out of the casino and stood breathing in the night air. He was dressed for a night out—dinner jacket, black bow tie, frilled shirt. All conventional stuff.

It was the man himself who drew my eyes. He was tall, over six foot, broad shouldered, long-legged, with a head of thick hair that was just on the edge of curling. He looked like someone who was used to living well. Everything about him spoke of a healthy animal who took the good things of life for granted and enjoyed them to the full.

He probably didn't have a brain in his head, but who cared?

Then I pulled myself together. It was men who'd got me into this mess, and now was no time to go misty-eyed over a handsome profile. I was getting a chill.

He came towards the bush behind which I was hiding, and I wondered if he was the one I should waylay and ask for help. The question was, did he have a 'Gina' in tow, ready to shoo me off? A man who looked like that probably did.

He came closer still, and stopped right by the bush.

Then he pounced.

I didn't see him coming, just felt his hands grasping me. One of them gripped hold of my ear, which hurt, so I lashed out at him as hard as I could.

I did pretty well. The high slit in the silver dress meant I could kick with some real force, so I did. I landed a few thumps on the shins, and from the yell he gave I might have caught him in a sensitive place as well.

'Come on out of there, you!' he said, gasping slightly. *'Oi!'*

That last one came from a punch in the midriff, and it seemed to decide him that the fight had gone on long enough because he tossed me onto my back and landed on top of me.

I'd been right about one thing. He *was* a healthy animal. I could feel it in every line of the big body pressed against mine as I lay looking up at him.

I couldn't see him so well now. There was a bright moon in the sky but his head came in between and his face was dark. I could only make out the glitter of his eyes and hear the sound of his breathing.

He was panting after his exertions, and I understood that, because so was I. Every part of me was suddenly warm and tingling, as though the struggle had got me really worked up. I could hear my heart thumping.

'Get off me,' I snapped.

'Good grief!' he said, peering at me more closely. 'What the devil—?'

'I said, get off me!'

He drew back and rose to his feet, pulling me up with him and keeping hold of my wrists.

'Who the hell do you think you are to jump

on me?' I demanded, trying to kick him again but not managing it this time.

'I'm a man who doesn't like being stolen from, even if it is just petty cash.'

'I haven't stolen from you,' I raged.

'But you were trying to. Why else were you hiding in the bushes? I've been crept up on before. I know the signs.'

'Oh, really?' I seethed. 'You're so clever, aren't you? But you've got it wrong this time.'

'Why are you soaking wet?' he asked suddenly.

'I've been swimming,' I flashed. 'I thought it would be good for my health. *Ow!*'

I'd actually managed to free one hand by then, but in the same moment I trod on something sharp.

I yelled and hopped about, and then found myself actually clutching him again to steady myself. That really annoyed me.

He was looking down at me with interest.

'You're not wearing very much,' he remarked.

'Ten out of ten for observation.'

'Well, I'm funny like that. When a girl's wet and half naked I tend to notice, especially up close.'

I abandoned politeness. 'Bully for you! And I am not a thief.'

'Well, you sure looked like one, skulking in the bushes until a victim came past. You think anyone who walks out of the casino must be a millionaire—'

It was madness to get into an argument with him, but I couldn't stop myself.

'Well, that's all you know,' I snapped. 'I've been in enough casinos to know that people walk out poorer than they go in. If they didn't, all the casinos would close down.'

'You really know the subject, don't you? I'll bet you have been in casinos! I expect your accomplice is still in there—'

'What accomplice?'

'The one who signalled you that I'd had a big win—'

'So you say! Every loser says he's a winner.'

'What do you think all that is on the ground?' he demanded, pointing down.

For the first time I realised that the ground was covered with notes.

'Those are my winnings, which just happened to fall out of my pocket while we were struggling,' he said.

'Don't try to make that sound like my fault,' I said. 'You pounced on me, not the other way around. I was not lurking to steal from you.'

'OK, we've exchanged pleasantries long

enough. Why don't you tell me what you're doing and why?'

'I am looking for the British Consul,' I asserted, with what I hoped was dignity.

'Dressed like that?'

'It's because I'm dressed like this that I need the Consul,' I said through gritted teeth.

'You need help, don't you?'

'You guessed!'

'I'm clever that way,' he said, not letting himself be offended by the edge in my voice, which I suppose was lucky for me.

'I'm running away,' I told him, 'but I've got nowhere to run to.'

'Where are you running from?'

'A yacht. It's called *The Silverado* and it's moored down there. Look.'

From here we could just about make out Vanner's yacht, far below us in the harbour.

'That one,' I said, 'right next to the big vulgar one.'

'You mean *The Hawk*?' he said.

'You know it?'

For a moment I thought he seemed uneasy.

'Why do you say it like that?' he asked.

'Like what?'

'As though knowing *The Hawk* is a crime. Are you acquainted with the owner?'

'I know of him. He's a creep called Jack

Bullen, and Hugh Vanner has been trying to crawl to him ever since he berthed.'

'That makes this Vanner character a creep, but why Bullen?'

'Because Vanner would only crawl to an even bigger creep than himself.'

'I suppose that's logical,' he admitted.

'He even sent him gold and diamond cuff-links. I ask you!'

'That's really disgusting. And who needs gold and diamonds? Look at these—'

He flashed his own cufflinks at me and I was startled. They were really rubbish, and I mean really. My family is expert in appraising jewellery and I absorbed it with my mother's milk.

Not that I needed expertise with these. They looked as if they'd come off a market stall, and the mother-of-pearl was peeling.

'You *do* know *The Hawk*, don't you?' I challenged him.

'In a sort of way,' he said vaguely.

I wondered if he was one of the ship's stewards, enjoying a night out. Despite his fancy shirt and bow tie this man was short of cash. His winnings probably represented a fortune to him.

'You'd better pick up your money,' I said.

'Can I risk letting you go?'

'I've got nowhere to run.'

He released my wrist and bent to grasp some of the notes.

'How about helping me?' he asked, looking up.

'I'd rather not touch your cash.'

'OK, OK, you're not a thief and I'm sorry I said it. Now, will you help me before a wind gets up and it blows away?'

I picked some up, deciding that my first thoughts had been right. Clearly this man needed every penny.

'So now tell me what you're doing here? Or can I guess? You're running from Vanner the creep?'

'Right! And from the other creeps that he wanted me to "be nice" to. This is his dress.'

His lips twitched.

'I'll bet he doesn't look as good in it as you.'

'Very funny. I jumped overboard to escape him, and now I don't know what to do or where to go. I need the Consul, but Monaco is so tiny it probably doesn't have one.'

'Yes, it does—well, a Vice-Consul anyway. If you like I'll take you to find him.'

I nearly collapsed with relief.

'Would you really? Thank you, thank you— could we go now, please?'

'All right. Just let me—'

'That's her!'

The voice came from the darkness, but it was followed at once by Vanner scurrying across the lawn like a black beetle.

'Get her!' he shrieked. *'Arrest her.'*

He was followed by two *gendarmes* who headed for me.

'Hold on a minute, there!'

The man from the casino spoke in a lazy voice, but there was something about him that stopped everyone in their tracks.

Vanner recovered first.

'This woman is a thief,' he shrieked. 'She stole money from me before leaving my boat. Look, she's holding it. That's mine. I demand that you arrest her.'

The *gendarmes* started to move again, but the man placed himself between them and me, and I realised again just how big he was. He could have dealt with two of them easily.

'The money's mine,' he said. 'This lady was helping me to pick it up. We hadn't finished, as you can see.'

He indicated the grass, where some stray notes still lingered.

'You're lying!' Vanner shrieked. 'The money's mine. She's a thief.'

'I suppose you're Hugh Vanner,' the man said, eyeing him with open contempt.

A new look, part caution, part suspicion, came over Vanner's face.

'How do you know who I am?'

'I recognise you from the description.'

This was kind of a private joke, since only he and I knew what that description had been. Vanner shot a look at me.

'What have you been saying about me?'

'That you're a low-life who tried to force me to sleep with your business buddies,' I said. 'That's why I had to jump overboard—'

'*With my money!*'

'Don't say that,' the man said quietly. 'I'm warning you, don't say it.'

'*You're* warning me? Who are you to tell me what to do?'

The man looked surprised. 'I'm Jack Bullen.'

It was worth anything to see Vanner's face at that moment. Even in the garden lights I could see him go green. This was the man he'd been trying to reach, to impress, and he'd met him like this.

Of course I knew there wasn't a word of truth in it. I'd given him the clue to dealing with Vanner and he'd taken it up brilliantly. And who was to know he wasn't really Jack Bullen, just as long so nobody saw his cuff-links?

'You're Jack Bullen?' Vanner said in a strangled voice that did me the world of good to hear.

'The one you sent the gold cufflinks to. Remember?'

Vanner gulped and began frantically back-pedalling with the *gendarmes,* assuring them that it was all a misunderstanding. They scowled at him, but finally departed.

'That's better,' Vanner said, trying to sound in command of the situation. 'Mr Bullen, you and me need to do some serious talking—'

'When you've returned this lady's property,' he said coolly.

'When I—?'

'Her clothes, her passport, and whatever you owe her in wages.'

'I suppose I'm well rid of her at that.'

'Deliver everything to *The Hawk*. That's where I'm going now.'

'Fine, fine. We can share a cab to the harbour—'

'No, we can't. Send those things over and don't keep me waiting.'

I couldn't see him well as he said this, but I had a good view of Vanner, and I saw the startling change that came over his face—a kind of withering. He'd seen something in this man's face that made him fall silent and take a step back.

The man took my arm and began to walk away.

'Wait a minute,' I whispered. 'You were going to take me to the Vice-Consul.'

'I've changed my mind. We're going to *The Hawk*.'

'Oh, no! Not another yacht. I've had enough of them to last a lifetime.'

I tried to pull away, but he wouldn't release my arm. He wasn't holding me all that tightly but there was no way I could escape.

He hailed a passing cab and almost tossed me into it.

'Now, look here—' I began.

'No, you look here. You can go with Vanner, with the *gendarmes*, or with me.'

'Or I can go to the Vice-Consul.'

'If you know where to find him. And just how long do you want to wander around dressed—or rather undressed—like that?'

'Are you daring to take advantage of my condition?'

'That's exactly what I'm doing.'

'That's blackmail.'

'It's what I'm good at. Now, shut up or I'll toss you back into the water.'

I opened my mouth to tell him what he could

do, but then shut it again. Not because I was afraid of his threats, or of him. I wasn't.

But I'd seen a gleam in his eyes that undermined his words. He was laughing, challenging me not to laugh with him, and despite everything I found myself doing so.

That was the moment when it all began.

CHAPTER TWO

Jack's Story

MOONLIGHT and roses. Trees waving gently in the Mediterranean breeze. Romantic music playing in the distance.

It was twenty-three-hundred hours and I was standing outside Monte Carlo Casino, ten grand richer than when I'd gone in.

Yes, that was the state I'd reached. Moonlight. Twenty-three-hundred hours. Ten grand.

But what else did you expect? I'm Jack Bullen. King Midas. Whatever I touch turns to ten grand. Or, if we're talking real money, ten million.

But tonight was only gambling, so I made do with pocket money.

I blame my grandfather, Nick, and his cuff-links. When he gave them to me he said they were lucky and they would help me win. And, dammit, he was right.

I don't win every single time. It's not quite

as bad as that. But I win often enough to come out richer. And it's all his fault.

I blame him for a lot more than that. Starting with my father. Nick was a happy-go-lucky fellow, who loved his family, earned enough from his little grocery business to get by, and enjoyed a laugh. So, according to Sod's Law, he was bound to have a son who thought he was feckless and worked night and day to 'better himself'.

I don't know if my father got better, but he certainly got richer. He started work in Grandpa's grocery and gradually took over, shunting his father aside. When he finally inherited the shop he built it into a chain, and raised me in the belief that my mission in life was to climb ever onward and upward to the glorious heights of tycoonery.

I'd rather have been a vet, and if Dad had lived longer I might have fought it out with him, but he died when I was fifteen and you can't argue with a dead man. Especially if he's left you everything.

Every last penny.

Which was unfair on my older sister, Grace, who was left to look after me, our mother being already dead. She didn't complain, because she'd picked up Dad's ideas about my dynamic future.

So I ended up doing business courses, computing, economics, just as if Dad were alive, because Grace said so.

As soon as I could touch my inheritance I transferred a fair share to her, but by that time it was too late. I was trapped in business and success.

Oh, yes, I was a success. I made money. The firm prospered. I bought another firm. Before I knew it I was a conglomerate.

I tried to lose money, I swear it. Don't even ask me how I ended up owning a cable television channel. It was a kind of accident. The channel showed light porn. The screen was always full of nubile girls wriggling around half dressed.

I changed all that. Out went the girls. In came animal programmes, stuff about vets, nature expeditions, deep-sea diving. I bought up the rights to old animal series that hadn't been seen for years, and the public loved it. Advertisers fought to give me their business.

Suddenly I was the wonder man whose finger on the public's pulse was never wrong, the visionary who could see past cheap smut to an audience starved of beauty, the marketing genius who could make wildlife profitable.

Actually, I just enjoyed animal programmes. It was like having a pact with the devil, only this devil was called Grandpa Nick. Wherever he was, he knew the terrible things money and success had done to me. I was out of my mind with boredom, and I swear sometimes I could hear the old man cackling.

There was nothing for me to do. Any fool can make money if they start out with a pile that someone else worked for.

Where were the great challenges in life?

At the moment my biggest challenge was fending off Grace's attempts to match me with Selina Janson. I usually ended up doing what Grace wanted because I felt so guilty at the way my life had been lived at the expense of hers.

It shouldn't have happened that way. She's only ten years older than me, and she could easily have married, especially after I struck out for myself.

When you fly the nest that's supposed to be it, right? You don't reckon on the nest flying after you.

But Grace nobly declared that nothing would make her abandon me, and I couldn't hurt her by saying how much I longed to be abandoned.

So here I was, mid-thirties and still officially sharing a home with my sister. I have my bachelor pad in town, and I'm there most nights, but Grace pretends it's just the odd occasion.

Maybe that was why she'd redoubled her efforts to marry me off to Selina.

'I don't know what you've got against that lovely girl,' she complained to me a few weeks earlier.

'I've got nothing against her,' I protested. 'I've never had anything against any of the girls you've tried to handcuff me to. But if I married every girl I've got nothing against, my wives would fill a city and there'd be some sort of scandal.'

'I do wish you'd be serious,' she fumed. 'It's no way to approach life.'

'It's a great way to approach not being married off against my will.'

'You've got to marry some time.'

'Why? For all you know I might be gay.'

'Don't give me that nonsense,' she snorted. 'Not after that girl who—'

'Yes, never mind,' I said hastily.

'You need a suitable partner in life, and you should be looking carefully.'

'Why? I've got you looking carefully for me,' I said, as lightly as I could.

As I knew she would, she missed the irony.

'Yes, I am, and it takes a lot of trouble to weed out the unsuitable ones.'

'Perhaps you shouldn't weed them out,' I said meekly. 'It would probably do me a lot of good to meet someone unsuitable, as an awful warning. It might really teach me a lesson.'

'Oh, stop playing the fool. I know all about the sort of semi-clad females who float through your apartment—'

How did she know? She never saw them. I'd made sure of that. But Grace had her spies and they could teach MI5 a thing or two.

I couldn't resist teasing her.

'They're not all semi-clad. Some of them wear nothing at—'

'That's enough. We're talking about your future wife.'

'I was trying not to talk about her. Why Selina?'

'Because she has the very best connections. Her mother's related to a title, her father's one of the richest merchant bankers in town—'

'And you think I'm so hard up that I need to marry money. Thanks!'

'Money should marry money. It doesn't pay to spread it around too thin.'

'Gracie, darling—'

'And don't call me, Gracie. It's vulgar.'

'We *are* vulgar. You talk as though we were heirs to an ancestral fortune, but Grandpa Nick made just enough to get by. Dad worked himself into the grave to make more than he needed, and, heaven help me, I'm going the same way. I'll swear I'm getting grey hairs.'

'Where?'

'Here at the side. Can you see?'

'No, I can't,' she said, giving me the fond smile that reminded me that I did actually like her a lot. 'You're too handsome for your own good, and you know it.'

'I'm still going grey from the treadmill I'm on. If I knew a way to jump off it I would, but I won't manage that by marrying Selina Janson.'

'I didn't mean to make too much of her money,' Grace said in a relenting tone. 'It's simply that she has all the right qualities.'

With difficulty I refrained from tearing my hair.

'No, Grace, she has only one of the right qualities, and that's the fact that I have nothing against her. It needs a lot more than that.'

She eyed me suspiciously.

'You haven't become entangled with some floozie, have you?'

'Why floozie?' I growled. 'I might have met a nice girl.'

'Then I'd know about her. Who is she?'

I was about to say that she didn't exist when some instinct for self-preservation stopped me.

'I don't think I ought to tell you any more

just now,' I said, choosing my words carefully.
'I don't want you investigating her to find out
if she's "suitable".'

'Meaning that she isn't?'

'She's suitable for me,' I said.

I accompanied the words with a smile which
was meant to be knowing, but I had a horrible
feeling I just looked foolish. I don't think Grace
noticed. She was seething at my mad dash for
independence.

'Surely you can tell me something about
her?' she demanded. 'What does she look
like?'

'She's beautiful.'

'What else?'

'She has a perfect figure and she's *very*
sexy,' I improvised wildly.

'Where did you meet her?'

'Around.'

'Really, this is very unsatisfactory.'

'Not to me,' I said.

'Well, I've made arrangements for the summer now, and it's too late to change them.'

The hairs began to stand up on the back o
my neck. 'What arrangements?'

'Oh, don't pretend not to know. We talke
about chartering a yacht and you agreed.'

'You vaguely mentioned a yacht,' I said

frantically searching my memory, 'but I don't think we actually agreed—'

'I said we should charter a yacht to cruise the Mediterranean and you said, 'Sure.' Which is what you always say. Raymond Keller is eager to join us. You said yourself he's bound to be the next president of Consolidated, and you can get him tied up while we're out at sea.'

'You've actually invited—?'

'Only in a vague sort of way. And there are one or two other contacts I'm working on—'

She rattled off a list of names and I had to admit they were well-chosen. All of them useful, all people I'd feel easy with and could make money out of. Grace knew her stuff, which was how she got away with being a bossy-boots.

I was beginning to feel almost relaxed about it when she said, 'And of course Selena will be there.'

'What do you mean, of course?'

'Well, the others will be couples, so naturally—'

I'll spare you the rest. Enough to say that I made a ritual protest, but gave in when I realised how I'd been backed into a corner. There wasn't a damned thing I could do about it without offending someone that it would be inconvenient to offend.

I just wish that some of the financial journalists could have been there to see. According to them I am Master of the Game, he whose will is law. Minions go in fear and trembling of my lightest word.

Hah!

They should have seen 'Bully Jack' cave in to Grace, that's all I can say.

Before I knew it everyone had accepted the invitations I'd never given, including Selina and her parents.

To protect myself, I issued a few invitations of my own. First there was Harry Oxton, who'd been trying to make an impression on Grace for a couple of years. He was a widower, a kindly man who put up with the way my sister used him when she needed an escort and forgot him at other times.

Then there were the newlyweds, Charles and Jenny Stover. I'd been their best man six months ago. When I explained to them that I needed their help, and exactly what kind of help I needed, they laughed and said fine!

Grace looked askance, though whether because Jenny was an old flame of mine or Charles was an old flame of Selina's I wouldn't like to say.

But I told her I'd invited them now and it

was too late to go back on it. She's not the only one who can do bland innocence.

But the one that really made her mad was Derek Lamming. His heart was set on Selina, and I think they'd have been married by now if Grace hadn't stuck her oar in, trying to secure Selina for me.

'You needn't think I don't know what you're up to,' Grace fumed to me.

'I'm sure you do,' I told her, grinning. 'But I learned deviousness from you, so naturally I'm good at it.'

'You do realise we don't have room for all the extra people you've invited, don't you?'

'Then we'll need a bigger yacht.'

That was how we exchanged the modestly luxurious vessel that Grace had chartered for the much larger *Hawk*.

What can I say about *The Hawk*? Think Onassis with knobs on. Other yachts had one swimming pool, *The Hawk* had two. It slept forty in over-the-top decadence.

Every cabin was done in a different style— French Second Empire, Roman villa, Egyptian splendour, Renaissance—all of them with solid gold accessories.

Since I was supposedly the big cheese of the outfit, I had a suite with a sunken bathroom, and a bed that could have slept ten.

Grandpa Nick would have laughed himself to stitches.

At the last minute Grace said worriedly, 'You won't do anything to offend Selina, will you?'

'Grace, I will be the perfect gentleman with Selina,' I vowed. 'I won't try to entice her into the moonlight, I won't ogle her in a swimsuit, in fact I won't even *look* at her in a swimsuit. I won't try to kiss her, or hold hands with her. I won't do one single thing that could compromise me into marriage with her. You can count on that.'

'All right, be difficult if you have to be. You know what I mean. I don't want to hear any more about this other woman—Cindy, or whatever her name is.'

'I never told you her name, and I'm not telling you now.'

'But you won't invite her to come along with us, will you?'

'No, I promise I'll confine my meetings with her to fleeting assignations wherever we drop anchor.'

Grace gave a scream, chiefly because she couldn't decide if I was serious or not. I decided to leave it that way. 'Cindy' might be useful.

I had no idea, then, just how useful.

We set off from Southampton and went across to Cherbourg on the first day, then across the Bay of Biscay and down the coast of Portugal to the Mediterranean.

We had a good time, with plenty of dinner and dancing, card-playing, wheeling and dealing—and flirting. I solved that problem by flirting madly with almost every woman aboard. Especially Jenny.

She was safe. I could romance her without fear of being hog-tied. But then Charles got a bit tense—actually said I was overdoing it. He responded by dancing smoochily with Selina for a whole evening. Then it was Jenny's turn to get tense.

They mended matters by vanishing into their cabin for three days, and emerging wreathed in smiles.

That was how I wanted to look when I found 'her'. It wasn't going to happen with Selina. I was beginning to wonder if it would happen with anyone.

In Gibraltar Charles and I managed to jump ship for a few hours, returning with the dawn. He spread tipsy hints about a lady I was supposed to have met ashore, then clapped his hand over his mouth as if realising that he'd said too much.

Grace gave me a look that would have shrivelled a lesser man.

We pulled the same stunt in Naples and Venice. Then it was time to start back down the Adriatic coast, with Grace snapping at me and demanding to know just how stupid I thought she was.

'If I thought you were stupid I'd be less scared,' I told her truthfully.

'Does this young woman really exist?' she demanded.

'My lips are sealed,' I replied solemnly.

'Then I think it's time we met her.'

'Is that the royal "we"?'

'No, it includes Selina, since you're playing fast and loose with the poor girl's feelings.'

'Grace, for the last time, I will not marry Selina. Is that understood?'

'We were talking about your lady-friend. Do tell me when you mean to produce her. Perhaps she'll be at the next port. You can bring her on board and we'll all have such a jolly time together.'

A master stroke. Game, set and match to Grace.

I had to produce a girl soon.

And Grace knew that I had nobody to produce.

Palermo, Naples, Genoa: all the way up the

coast I ducked and dived, with Grace asking, with unbearable sweetness, when she would have the pleasure of meeting my 'friend'.

When we anchored at Monte Carlo there were still several days left to go, which filled me with gloom. I was wondering how I could arrange an urgent call home and high-tail it out of there.

The day after we arrived I received an unexpected gift. It was a set of solid gold diamond-studded cufflinks, and they came from a man called Hugh Vanner, on *The Silverado*, anchored just next door.

I couldn't wait to get rid of them. I'd vaguely heard of Vanner. He was the kind of shifty character who hung around on the fringe of the legitimate business world, picking up what he could get. His methods were those of a slimeball. I sent the cufflinks back with a note saying that I didn't accept gifts from strange men. It was a safe bet that he wouldn't get the joke.

We all went to the casino. It was a sedate visit, during which we all behaved sedately and lost sedate amounts of money, then returned to the ship consoling each other for losses that we would barely notice.

Once back on board we all went to our cabins, prior to congregating for a nightcap. I was feeling a bit tense, because Selina had been making significant remarks all evening and I could feel the noose tightening.

The last straw came when a steward informed me that Vanner had called the ship while I was away.

Now I was really paranoid. Looking out, I saw lights on *The Silverado*, and I had sudden visions of him coming over. I'd been hunted as much as I could stand, and suddenly I went mad.

'Tell the Captain to have the boat ready to take me ashore again,' I said. 'And keep quiet about it.'

Before leaving I changed my cufflinks. It was a chance to test a theory. I'd worn platinum cufflinks for the first visit to the casino, and lost. Now I was wearing Grandpa's old tatty ones.

My luck turned the moment I went in. I won until I got bored with winning, then strolled out into the gardens. At once I knew I was being stalked.

My boredom with money doesn't extend to giving it to people who are trying to pilfer it, so I made my move first, pouncing on whoever was crouching in the bushes.

Suddenly I was grappling with a whirling dervish who thumped and kicked with alarming force and precision. The last one caught me straight in the midriff and almost winded me. It was sheer desperation that made me toss the other party to the ground and dive on top.

And there was approximately ninety pounds of slender female writhing beneath me. If I hadn't been gasping already I had plenty to gasp about now. In self-defence I got to my feet.

The next few minutes were par for the course. I accused her of trying to steal from me; she denied it. But I was talking off the top of my head. My real consciousness was elsewhere, in the urgent warmth that had seized me as I lay on top of her and wouldn't let go of me now.

It got worse when I realised something else about her.

'Why are you soaking wet?' I asked.

'I've been swimming,' she said scathingly. 'I thought it would be good for my health. *Ow!*'

She'd trodden on something sharp, which must have hurt because her feet were bare. So was the rest of her, almost.

She was wearing a silver lacy dress, tight at the waist and slit high at the thigh. The water not only made it cling to her, it also made it virtually transparent. So now I could see what had been writhing against me.

She was beautiful—slender, perfectly proportioned, rounded, dainty, sexy, provocative. This was getting very difficult.

Make me strong, I prayed silently to the guy who helps me on these occasions. *Let me at least act like a gentleman, even if I don't feel like one right now.*

But he must have been off-duty tonight, because there was the warmth, growing stronger every moment.

I returned to normal consciousness to discover that we were having an infuriated discussion about casinos. I think I accused her of having an accomplice inside, but don't ask me how we reached that point. I know we ended up scrabbling around on the ground for the cash that had fallen out of my pocket in the struggle.

I suppose it was when she mentioned the British Consul that I realised I'd got it wrong, and she really wasn't a thief.

'Where are you running from?' I asked.

'A yacht. It's called *The Silverado* and it's moored down there. Look.' She pointed down into the harbour. 'That one. Right next to the big vulgar one.'

'You mean *The Hawk*?' I asked cautiously.

'You know it?' Now she definitely sounded hostile.

'Why do you make that sound like a crime?' So she told me all about *The Hawk*, how its boss was a creep called Jack Bullen, better known as Bully Jack.

I was glad she couldn't see me too well at that moment.

'Hugh Vanner has been trying to crawl to him,' she seethed.

'That makes this Vanner character a creep,' I said, 'but why Bullen?'

'Because Vanner would only crawl to an even bigger creep than himself. He even sent him gold and diamond cufflinks. I ask you!'

'That's really disgusting,' I agreed fervently.

She told me how Vanner had tried to make her be 'nice' to his guests, and she'd jumped overboard to escape him.

She was small and defenceless, with not a single possession—not on her, anyway. But she was defying the world and I'd never seen anything like her.

Maybe the idea came to me then. Or maybe it had been nudging the edges of my thoughts for a few minutes past. But it was forming rapidly, and I had the outline pretty much shaped when I heard, *'That's her!'*

And there was a man who could only have been Vanner, rushing at us with two *gendarmes*, shrieking that the silver girl had stolen from him.

I pointed out that the money lying all around

us was mine, which stymied him, although he still frothed at the mouth until, to shut him up, I had to give him my name.

'You're Jack Bullen?' he said in a choked voice.

After that he couldn't get rid of the *gendarmes* fast enough. He wanted to get me alone to do some business schmoozing.

'When you've returned this lady's property,' I told him. 'Deliver everything to *The Hawk*.'

Fending off his attempts to join us, I took her arm and made for the road where there would be a taxi.

'You were going to take me to the Vice-Consul,' she said.

'I've changed my mind. We're going to *The Hawk*.'

She was still arguing as we got into the taxi. I laid out her options.

'You can go with Vanner, with the *gendarmes* or with me.'

'That's blackmail.'

'It's what I'm good at. Now, shut up or I'll toss you back into the water.'

I don't normally talk to women like that, but something had happened to me that night. I was like a drowning man who sees his last hope and knows he has to grasp it. So my finesse went out of the window.

Then I saw her looking at me. An incredulous, half-quizzical smile had taken over her face, and I found myself smiling back. We knew nothing about each other, except that we were on the same wavelength.

'All right,' she said.

CHAPTER THREE

Della's Story

'WE DON'T have much time,' the man told me in a low, hurried voice.

I could see that we didn't. The taxi was on its way down the slope to the harbour, and we were going to be there at any moment.

'All I can say now,' he said, 'is that I need help badly, and you're the only person who can give it to me.'

'How?'

'I'm being nudged—well, frog-marched—into a marriage I don't want to make. Selina's a banker's daughter, and money must marry money. That sort of thing.'

'Sure, like you're a millionaire,' I said sceptically.

'I told you who I am. Jack Bullen.'

'Yes, after I'd given you all the clues. That story will do well enough for Vanner, but not me. I suppose you work on his yacht?'

'I beg your pardon?'

'Honestly, I'm grateful to you for saving me, but I wasn't born yesterday. The silver plate's wearing off those cufflinks, and I'll bet you borrowed the flash clothes from your boss.'

He tore his hair, and I had to admit that the tousled look suited him.

'I haven't got time to argue,' he said. 'Look, this is the harbour, and there's a boat ready to take us to *The Hawk*. Just act like you're wildly in love with me, and you might save me from a fate worse than death.'

He was mad, but I owed him a lot, so I reckoned I'd play along. I was feeling light-headed by then, and willing to let the night end any way it would.

He paid off the cab and we headed towards a small boat that was waiting. The pilot greeted us with a wave.

'Evening, Pete.'

'Evening, Mr Bullen.'

I was too astounded to speak until I was settled into the boat.

'He called you—'

'Well, I told you,' he said, sounding aggrieved.

I tried to see his face as we sped out to the deep water where *The Hawk* was moored. But the light changed so fast that I couldn't make out much except that he was grinning like a man with a handful of aces. I knew that look. I even had a weakness for it. And already I was getting warning signals that I was determined to ignore.

One thing was clear. This man was trouble and fun in equal measures.

So let the good times begin!

'Just say that you'll help me,' he said urgently.

'How?'

'By being my girlfriend. Here's the story. We've known each other for a few months, we meet constantly at my London flat, and these last few weeks we've had secret assignations all over Europe. My sister keeps demanding to meet you because she doesn't think you exist, but you do.'

He was gabbling, and I only took half of it in.

'Assignations all over Europe—' I said. 'Weren't we travelling together?'

'No, I was on the yacht.'

'Why didn't you invite me on the yacht, you cheapskate?'

'Because Grace wouldn't have you.'

'Grace?'

'My sister. My keeper. She's organised this trip to get me married, but you are going to thwart her.'

'So—I'm your girlfriend—?'

'That's right. I'm mad about you because you're beautiful, sweet-natured, witty, and the sexiest thing in creation. Do you think you can remember that?'

'Can *you?*' I asked.

'Yes, all of it. Especially the last bit. OK, we're nearly there. Act the part.'

'You want me to gaze into your eyes?'

'I think it'll take a bit more than that,' he said hoarsely, and wrapped his arms tightly around me.

I ought to have seen it coming, but he moved so fast that I was taken by surprise. Suddenly I was being pressed back against the curve of his arm while his mouth covered mine in a perfect simulation of hungry passion.

He was clever. I'll give him that. Nothing offensive. Considering that I was half naked and we'd only just met, it was a virtuous kiss: everything for show on the outside and nothing really happening—except deep inside me, where there was a whole lot happening.

I put my arms around him and helped out with the performance. At least I told myself it was just a performance. There was something about being pressed against him that made me tend to forget that.

I was dimly aware that the boat had stopped

and the pilot was turning around from the front to regard us.

'Er—sir—?' he said, grinning.

Jack Bullen waved him away and redoubled his efforts. It seemed only polite to co-operate, so I did, writhing my fingers in his hair and pressing against him. There were lights on us now, so I gave it all I'd got.

Looking up over his shoulder, I could see men and women leaning over the rails to gape down at us. They were all wide-eyed. Two women especially—one young, one middle-aged—glared at us with undisguised fury.

He drew back his head a little and whispered, 'Are they watching us?'

'With their eyes on stalks,' I murmured back.

'Good. Let's make it worth their while.'

He returned to the fray, but this time in a way that was even more self-consciously theatrical. He kissed my face, my neck, all the way down, then below my ears.

'Enough?' he asked.

'I think you've made your point,' I said with difficulty.

'Then let's go,' he muttered.

As I climbed up the gangway ahead of him I was acutely conscious of my semi-naked behind waving about just in front of his eyes. I ought to have been modestly shocked, and with

Vanner I would have been. But with Jack Bullen I could only remember the feel of his body pressing mine into the warm earth behind the casino. I wondered if he was enjoying the view. I had to take a deep breath against the wave of self-consciousness that washed over me, and then I found myself stumbling.

He was there at once, his hands grasping my hips, steadying me.

'Are you all right?' he asked.

'Yes—yes, I'm fine,' I gabbled, wondering if I would ever make sense again. My insides were reacting in a way that was all their own.

We reached the deck and I got a better look at our audience. The men were in dinner jackets and the women glittered with costly jewels. There was no doubt about it now. I'd fallen into a den of millionaires.

They were taking a good look at me, too. Jack put his arm about my shoulders, turned to the middle-aged woman who looked as if she'd swallowed a lemon, and said firmly, 'Grace, this is…Cindy.'

If looks could kill she would have slaughtered us both on the spot. But mostly me.

'Well, this is a pleasure,' she said. 'At last. Even if a somewhat unexpected, not to mention delayed, pleasure.'

'You'll have to forgive the delay,' he said. 'We've been rather wrapped up in each other.'

Grace was looking me up and down in a way that made me very conscious that my neck was cut low and my skirt was slit high, and that was all there was.

'I trust you've had a pleasant evening?' she said, with a little smirk.

'She's had a misfortune,' he said quickly, saving me from having to answer. 'She had to leave her ship suddenly. Her things will be arriving at any moment, but in the meantime I'm taking her below before she gets pneumonia.'

He whisked me away, giving nobody the chance to say anything.

If I'd had any lingering doubts about who he was they were quelled as soon as I saw his cabin—although *suite* would be a better word. The decor was vaguely ancient Roman, and the last word in luxury. There was a bathroom with a sunken bath, and taps that looked like solid gold.

A quick inspection proved that they really were. I told you, I'm an expert on these things.

'Mr Bullen—?'

'After what went on in the boat, don't you think you should call me Jack?'

'Jack—and, by the way, you should have warned me that my name is Cindy.'

'It isn't. That's just what Grace calls you. I'm afraid she means it as a put-down. What's your real name?'

'Della Martin.'

'Fine.' He pointed at my dress. 'Take that off—quickly.'

'I beg your pardon?'

'Before you catch your death of cold.' He took a large white towelling robe from the closet. 'Then have a hot bath and put this on.'

'Lovely,' I said, shivering. 'I can't get over this place. I thought you were poor.'

'Does that matter? You think I need help less than a poor man? I need it more. If I didn't have any money I wouldn't have a problem. Selina's father is a banker, and they all want me to make an ''alliance'' with the family. I'm trapped. What can I do? I don't want to be outright rude.'

'Why not?'

He sighed.

'I'm not very good at it,' he admitted, sounding slightly ashamed. 'Not with Grace, anyway. She keeps reminding me that she's been my second mother. It's easier to play dumb and let her realise gradually that she's wasting her time. So now you're my best hope—my *only* hope.'

'She isn't going to be easily fooled.'

'She never was,' he said with a reminiscent sigh.

As if to prove it there was a step outside and the sound of someone trying to open the locked door. Then his sister's voice.

'Jack, open this door at once. We have to talk.'

'Not just now, Grace,' he called back. 'We'll talk later.'

'I said now.' The lock rattled again. 'Open this door at once.'

'Goodnight, Grace.'

This time there was iron in his voice, and anyone else would have been deterred by it. But not her.

'I'm not going away until we've had this out,' she called. 'You may think you've got me fooled, but I don't believe a word about this woman who's appeared so conveniently. She's probably some cheap little waitress you picked up somewhere. *Open this door!*'

He ground his teeth. My temper was rising. I'd never disliked anyone so much after such a short time as I did this woman.

'Goodnight, Grace,' he called again.

'Open this door!'

'That's it,' I muttered. 'Now I'm mad. It's time for action.'

He looked nervous. 'Are you going to be violent?'

'If necessary. Come here!'

I reached for him, hooking my arm about his neck, drawing him very close, very fiercely. He barely had time to draw breath, but after that I think I managed to make him forget about breathing. When we parted he was gasping.

'I hope I'm never the one you're mad at,' he managed to say.

'Shut up!'

I returned to the action, but this time I freed one hand and unlocked the door, so that Grace came marching in to find us wrapped in each other's arms.

I did it purely out of expediency. He'd been good to me, and I was going to be good to him. It had nothing whatever to do with the way he'd kissed me in the boat. I was *not* looking for an excuse to do it again.

And you can believe that or not—as you like.

With the audience being closer this time, we had to make it look realistic, and he really worked at that. I could feel his hands roving all over me, and I wondered how much more my nervous system could stand in one evening.

Grace, I'm happy to say, nearly went ballistic. She stood there yelling, 'Will you stop this and listen to me?'

I don't know how long she kept it up. Everything was fuzzy, and I was only vaguely aware when she stopped abruptly and a man's voice said, *'Jack!'*

We managed to disengage ourselves, and I saw a young man and woman whom I'd vaguely noticed on deck. Now, as then, they were holding hands. They seemed to come as a pair.

'There's someone to see you, Jack,' the young man said, standing aside so that we could all see Vanner.

'Thanks, Charles,' Jack said.

Vanner was managing a rough version of a smile, as if he still hoped to get some sort of profit out of this. He kept the smile riveted in place as he held out a brown envelope to me.

'Here's your passport and your wages, plus a bonus that I think you'll find generous.'

I checked the passport and was relieved to see that it was actually mine.

'I brought your bags too,' Vanner said. 'I left them on deck.'

He turned his frayed smile on Jack. 'Mr Bullen—'

'Get out,' Jack said.

'I just hoped that—now things are sorted out—you and I could—'

Jack spoke in a voice of steel. 'I said, get out. Are you deaf?'

Vanner drew a sharp breath, and again there was that withered look on his face, as though he were suddenly filled with fear. But then fear was driven out by the spoilt petulance of a thwarted child.

'I see,' he snapped, glaring at me. 'In that case, now I've returned your property, I'll have *mine*!'

He pointed at the silver dress. I backed away from him and put out my hand.

'It's mine,' he bellowed. 'I paid for it.'

'Oh, give it to him,' Jack said in disgust. 'Don't let him have any excuse to make more trouble.'

He picked up the towelling robe again, and shooed me into the bathroom. Once in there I stripped off and put on the robe, which almost swallowed me up. When I returned Vanner had resumed arguing in a way that he probably thought was persuasive. Phrases reached me'

'Understand these things—men of the world—lot in common—'

'Not that much in common,' I heard Jack say in a bored tone. 'No young lady has ever felt she needed to risk her life to escape me.'

I tossed the dress at Vanner. I couldn't bear to get any closer to him.

'The steward will see you off the boat,' Jack said.

'No, I'll do it,' said the young man he'd addressed as Charles. 'It'll be a pleasure.'

He and the girl followed Vanner up to the deck, leaving me below with Jack and Grace, and someone else who had appeared. She was about my age, and beautiful in a chilly way. She was one of the women I'd seen looking down at me a few minutes earlier, and I didn't need a crystal ball to tell me this was Selina.

She looked me up and down, then down and up, and I could tell what she thought about the robe, which was too big everywhere, so that I had to clutch it around me. I hoped someone would bring my clothes down soon.

'I think I'll have a bath,' I said, with as much dignity as I could muster.

I turned back to the bathroom, but before I could go in there was a commotion from above—shouting, then the sound of something landing in the water. A moment later Charles came running back.

'The lousy so-and-so!' he said. 'He just grabbed your bags from the deck and tossed them overboard. They sank at once.'

'*Oooooh!*' It was meant as an exclamation

of annoyance, but it came out as a despairing wail. 'Why does this keep happening to me? Why can't everything go right for once? What have I done to deserve this? What am I going to wear?'

'Oh, please don't worry about that,' said the cool beauty at once. 'I have plenty of things you can borrow.'

'Thanks, Selina,' Jack said.

He sounded surprised at what seemed like good nature, but I'd noticed the look she gave Grace, which said they needed to talk urgently. They sailed out together.

I shot into the bathroom. My teeth were chattering and I'd had enough for one night.

There was a whole collection of potions to tip into the bath, some of them definitely feminine, so I guessed they came with the yacht. I found one with a lovely smell and poured it into the running water until the place was all over suds. Lovely!

Oh, the bliss of sinking down into them! They were warm, they were everywhere, they were making me human again.

The door opened slowly and Jack's head appeared.

'Permission to come in?' he asked.

'Sure,' I said sleepily.

With the suds right up to my neck I was

decent, although by now I was past caring. The world was turning into a pleasant fuzz, in which I actually felt safe for the first time since for ever.

So I just gazed sleepily as he came and sat down on the floor by the sunken bath, carefully depositing a bottle of champagne and two glasses.

'I've ordered some food for you as well,' he said, 'but I thought we should celebrate together first.'

I gave him a sleepy smile. 'What are we celebrating? Not that it matters.'

'Your escape,' he said. 'My escape. But you're right. Who cares? Celebrate because you feel like it. It's the only good reason.'

He handed me a full glass and I savoured every drop. It was the very finest, and when I'd drained the glass I held it out for a refill.

When he'd finished pouring, he stopped, looked me straight in the eyes. I knew why. We'd met in a whirlwind and hadn't stopped spinning since. This was our first chance to consider each other at leisure.

So, while he considered me I considered him, and I liked what I saw. He'd removed his jacket and his bow tie, leaving a snowy white dress shirt, open at the throat, showing just the hint of a hairy chest.

I have a weakness for hairy chests.

He was tall, and constructed in a way that shouted 'virile'. I'd already discovered that, in one sense, but it was interesting seeing it as well. I supposed he spent most of his time behind a desk, but he must work out every day.

There wasn't an ounce of fat on him, but he looked as if he lived well. He had that glow that money brings. I've had it myself from time to time. His hair was dark brown, slightly curly, with a faint touch of red that you had to look very close to see.

His mouth was like his body, in that I knew it well while seeing it properly for the first time. Now I saw it, I understood its effect on me. It was generous and curved, yet firm.

His eyes were the dark brown of bitter chocolate, very deep and intense. Their gleam came and went without warning. It was there now. When he smiled I smiled back, which made him smile even more. There was no need for words.

'Are you all right?' he asked.

'Yes, thank you.' I sighed. 'For the first time in weeks, I'm all right. Thanks to you.'

I stretched a leg luxuriously, raising it out of the water, all sleek and sudsy. Then I put it down again quickly, remembering.

'Please don't do that,' he begged. 'I'm trying

to be a gentleman, although after the evening we've had— But don't worry, I'm on my best behaviour. Do you realise that I know nothing about you?' he hurried on. 'Except that you came out of the water, all silver and shining like a mermaid. Are you married?'

'No.'

'Engaged? Promised?'

'Nothing. Nobody,' I said briefly.

'There's nobody who's going to appear suddenly, yelling, "She's mine!"?'

I raised an eyebrow at him. 'You left it a bit late to worry about that, didn't you?'

He grinned. 'So I did. But you wouldn't like to think of me shaking in my shoes for fear of the man in your life, would you?'

'I don't think I could ever imagine you shaking in your shoes,' I said. 'More likely to make other people shake.'

He grinned again. It had an unsettling quality.

'I'm harmless, I promise. To you, anyway. But seriously, is there anyone you want to call to say where you are?'

Various members of my family flitted through my mind: my aunts and uncles, cousins. No need to bother them. They had their own problems. Finally I thought of Grandad, and decided that where he was he didn't need any more trouble.

'Nobody,' I said.

'So, come on, tell me something about yourself.'

I thought about all I could have told him, which was a lot. He wouldn't like it. There was much about my life, my past, that even I didn't like.

'Perhaps the less you know about me the better,' I mused. 'I'm just here to fit into the part you want me to play.'

'But you're still a person in your own right,' he said. 'You don't just exist for my convenience.'

Oh, hell's bells! Do you know how hard it is to get a man to think like that? And when I finally met one he had to be a ship that was going to pass in the night. Life just wasn't fair!

'I think, for a while, you need me to exist for your convenience,' I said cautiously. 'I am Cindy, and my past is whatever you tell me it is.'

'Is that your way of telling me to mind my own business?' he asked, with his head on one side.

'If I tell you that I'm a hundred per cent with you, and I won't let you down, what else do you need to know?'

'Nothing.'

'In that case—' I laid my finger over my mouth.

'Good. OK, here's the deal. I'm employing you—for a length of time to be decided later. Your job is to convince Grace that she's wasting her time. I shall provide a complete wardrobe, a generous salary, and anything else necessary for you to be convincing. Now, I'll leave you before your suds start to fade. When you've finished there'll be a meal waiting for you next door.'

He closed the door, leaving me to my thoughts.

I refused to think of the problems that might lie ahead. For the moment things were looking good, and if there's one thing I've learned in my colourful and sometimes bizarre, existence, it's to take life as it comes.

I leaned back, sipping champagne.

CHAPTER FOUR

Della's Story

I WAS drowning. Perfumed suds were going up my nose and I was floundering about, submerged in water, not knowing where I was, getting scared.

Just in time a pair of hands grasped me and hauled me out of the water.

'What happened?' I choked, sending suds everywhere.

'You must have fallen asleep and slid underwater,' Jack gasped.

I had a violent coughing fit, clinging to him for dear life, too frightened by what had nearly happened to care that I was naked. Jack had climbed into the bath with me, and now he was sodden, his shirt transparent. Without letting go of me, he reached out and pulled the plug so that the water drained away.

'Thank goodness you came in,' I spluttered.

'I nearly didn't. I called something through the door. When you didn't reply I got worried, but I didn't know what to do. I felt kind of shy about bursting in on you.'

If I hadn't been recovering I might have said something like, *In a pig's eye, you were shy!* The one thing this man could never be was shy with a naked woman. But I held my tongue. After all, he'd just saved me for the second time that evening.

'I must have fallen asleep,' I said. 'Another moment and—' I shuddered.

'Let's get you out of here.' He hauled me out of the bath so that I could sit on the carpet, then tossed the robe over me and headed for the door

'Selina's sent you some of her clothes,' he said over his shoulder. 'I'll hand them through.'

A moment later the door opened. His hand appeared, dropped a bag on the floor, and re-treated.

If they were Selina's clothes, I was a monkey's uncle. She must have had a maid with her, and this was one of her uniforms—grey, shapeless and too big.

It was a declaration of war.

Fine! If that was what she wanted, I was up for it.

I opened the bathroom door and called out, 'Are you ready for this?'

'Yes,' he called back.

Without a word I walked out and presented myself to him, turning very slowly so that he could view the dress in all its ghastliness, while his eyes popped and his jaw dropped.

'I don't know what to say,' he said at last. 'Except that I'm sorry.'

I'd recovered my sense of humour by this time. 'I suppose you could see this as a positive sign,' I pointed out. 'It means she's taking me seriously, which is what you want.'

'That's the spirit. And I'll buy you a new wardrobe tomorrow.'

Jack had also changed, since his clothes had got wet. Now he was in casuals, but he still managed to look as though he owned the world.

I don't know what I ate, I was too tired and hungry to care. Jack served me himself, as tenderly as a mother, eating little and always watching out for my needs.

'More champagne?' he asked me once.

'I could murder a cup of tea,' I said.

He was on the phone to the kitchens at once. Just as he finished there was a knock at the door. He was scowling as he went to open it, but he smiled when he saw who it was.

'Jenny, Charles—come in.'

It was the man and girl I'd seen holding

hands on deck, and then later when they showed Vanner below.

'We're not disturbing anything, are we?' the girl asked, coming in and smiling at me.

'Not a thing,' I said, liking her at once. She was in her twenties, very pretty, with real warmth in her smile.

I liked her even more when I learned why she'd come.

'We're the same size,' she said, opening a bag and showing me the contents. 'So I brought you some of my clothes. I thought Selina would try something, and I can see she has.'

'Bless you, Jenny,' Jack said.

I blessed her too when I saw the clothes. They were beautiful, and they fitted.

Jenny was a darling. She could see that I was almost asleep, and she took Charles away quickly.

'You need some sleep,' Jack said. 'Get to bed.'

'What about you?'

'I'll sleep on the floor.'

I looked at the bed. It was vast.

'That seems a bit unfair,' I mused.

'There are some spare pillows I could put down the centre,' he offered.

'Sounds a good idea.'

It didn't seem such a good idea when I

looked at the nightdress Jenny had brought me. It was nightwear for a bride, low at the front and transparent everywhere. It forced me to reconsider the situation.

Jack undressed in the bathroom. When he returned and saw me dressed for the night, his eyebrows went up. I looked awful—shapeless and sexless. But that was probably a good thing.

'Don't tell me Jenny brought you that old sack?'

'No, this comes from Selina's maid. Jenny's nightdress wouldn't fit me.'

'But you must be the same—'

He stopped quickly and I saw his face change as he realised that there was more to this than being the same size.

'Yes,' he said. 'Yes—right—'

He was actually turning pink, which I reckoned didn't happen very often.

He had some trouble finding his pyjamas, which puzzled me until I realised that he probably didn't wear them much. They were white silk, and he looked just as good in them as he had in everything else. They were also semi-transparent, which might have been why he got into bed quickly, looking even pinker.

I climbed in the other side, wishing I could have worn Jenny's sexy nightie. In these surroundings, and getting into bed with a man whose body I already knew so incongruously well, it would have been the right thing to wear. And if it did leave me half naked—well, he was getting used to that too.

I reasoned it wouldn't have been fair to give him the wrong impression. Hell! What wrong impression? We'd got past that stage in the first five minutes.

So here I was, lying in bed with the sexiest man I'd ever met, with a pillow between us, trying desperately to think pure thoughts.

It was very, very difficult.

I wondered if he was having the same trouble.

Perhaps not, since he'd just seen me dressed in sackcloth and looking like King Kong's mother.

Pity!

Don't get me wrong. I'm not a prude, no matter what previous events might suggest. I've lived around some very charming people. Too charming, some of them, and they could leave you wishing you hadn't listened to a word they'd said. But it had been fun while it lasted.

I'm not what Vanner thought, but I like do fellers. I flirt and fool around, dress to catch their eye, and when I've done that—well, things happen. Nice things.

Unfortunately my romances have tended to be very short-lived, for reasons I can't go into here. But I knew a fantastic guy when I found myself in bed with him, even with a pillow between us.

'All right to turn out the light?' he asked, in a voice that I thought sounded tense.

'Yes, fine,' I said.

He turned it out and for a while we both lay in the darkness, listening to each other's breathing.

I had a problem. I usually slept naked, and the sackcloth I was wearing made me as hot as fire. Well, something did, anyway. And I began to sense that it was the same for him, if his movements were anything to go by. He tossed and turned and finally pulled off his pyjama jacket.

So then I had to start thinking pure thoughts all over again.

But I had my moment. Half an hour later, after a lot more fretful tossing around, he suddenly leapt out of bed and shot into the bathroom as though all the devils in hell were after him. A moment later I heard the unmistakable sound of a shower.

I slept happily after that.

* * *

I awoke first, in the early light, and propped myself up to look at him.

He looked fantastic asleep, even with a night's growth of beard. It was thick, dark, and gave him the air of a pirate.

He was bare-chested, not having replaced the pyjama jacket. I wondered what else he hadn't replaced, but from here I couldn't see. What I could see was that he really did have a hairy chest. Rich and curly. Just as I like it.

He opened his eyes.

'Hi,' he said. Then he became aware of his chest. 'Sorry about this. I just—'

He was interrupted by a knock on the door, followed by a cheery voice calculated to freeze the blood.

'Coo-ee! Is anyone awake?'

'Oh, Lord, it's Grace,' he said desperately.

'I've brought your coffee,' came the voice through the door. 'Can I come in?'

'Just a minute, Grace,' he yelled. 'I'm not decent.' Under his breath he muttered, 'Where is it? Where is it?'

'What?'

'My jacket. Oh, there it is on the floor.'

He leaned down to scoop it up, accidentally revealing the answer to the question that had been troubling me. He'd probably left them in the bathroom.

Inspiration seized me and I grabbed the pyjama jacket from his hands, tossing it back onto the floor.

'Are you crazy?' he hissed.

'No, but you are,' I told him. 'You're supposed to be nuts about me, *and you're sleeping in that?* Come on—make it look real.'

As I spoke I was pulling the pillow out of the bed, tossing it away, then stripping off the sack and pushing it down the bed where nobody could see it.

'Push the sheet down to your waist,' I said, and when he did so I put my arm around his neck, trying not to be too aware of the length of his naked body against mine. '*Now* we look real.'

His eyes gleamed. 'That's the spirit.' He raised his voice. 'OK, Grace.'

I don't know exactly what Grace had expected to see, but it must have been a lot less than what she did see—because she looked as if she'd swallowed a hedgehog, prickles and all. I nestled against Jack, smiling at her as she stood there with a small tray bearing two coffees.

I'll say this for her: she got her act together fast, fixed her smile on with steel rivets, and approached the bed.

'I hope you two slept well,' she said, like any hostess greeting any guest in the morning.

'Well,' I mused, 'I wouldn't exactly say slept. But it was a *wonderful* night.'

As I finished I gave an inane little giggle, and, if I say so myself, I do 'inane' very well. I have a large repertoire of giggles, to be produced on demand, but the jewel in the crown is definitely 'inane'.

It got to Grace, anyway. The smile slipped, but she forced it back into place.

'I'm so glad you find everything satisfactory,' she said, straight out of the hostess's etiquette book.

'It was very satisfactory,' I breathed.

Beside me I felt Jack grow tense and turn his head so that his face was hidden against my shoulder. He was fighting not to laugh.

'Thanks for the coffee, Grace,' he said, looking up at last. 'Perhaps we'll have breakfast in here, too.'

'Impossible,' she declared. 'You can't insult your guests like that.'

'I think they'll understand—' Jack started to say.

'Nonsense. Of course you must come to breakfast,' she declared. 'I shall tell them to expect you in half an hour.'

She sailed out, closing the door very firmly behind her.

'Wow!' I said.

'You see my problem?'

Actually, I was being distracted by another problem just then. He was pressing closer to me, his hip against my leg, and there was no doubting what I could feel.

'Yes.' He groaned, meeting my eyes. 'Look, I apologise. I meant to— I mean, I didn't mean to— Oh hell!'

'I understand,' I assured him solemnly. 'But we're expected for breakfast.'

'Hell again!'

'Well, it's your fault,' I complained. 'Why do you let her order you about? You're the Big Man—'

'Do you mind not putting it like that?' he asked faintly.

'You know what I mean. You're supposed to be master of all you survey. Just tell her that you'll do things your way. Are you a man or a mouse?'

'Of all the stupid questions,' he said explosively. 'I'm a mouse, of course. How else do you think I got into this mess?'

'Well, Grace has spoken, so we'll have to postpone this—er—interesting discussion until another day.'

'Yes,' he said delicately. 'Look, I'm going to have to make a dash for the bathroom.'

'Cold shower?'

'Freezing.'

'Don't use all the icy water.'

He grinned and began to slide out of the bed. Then he stopped.

'I've lost my pyjama bottoms. So do you mind closing your eyes until I reach the bathroom?'

'Sure thing.'

'And no peeking. Promise me that.'

'Of course I promise,' I said, shocked to the core by his doubts. 'What do you take me for? I give you my solemn word—not one tiny peek.'

But I lied, my friends, I lied. Oh, how gloriously I lied!

Breakfast was on the sundeck, under a blue awning. I'll swear the whole boat was there to watch us arrive. Word had gone around, and any of the sailors and staff who could possibly find an excuse to be there were hovering, trying to look indifferent.

The guests didn't even try. Their eyes bored into us as we appeared on deck and made our way to the table. I was wearing a pair of elegant dark green trousers and a fawn silk blouse that

Jenny had loaned me, and I was really grateful to her.

Every woman there wore couture, even at this hour of the morning. It was casual, of course, but the kind of casual that costs a bomb, and Jenny's clothes made me look as though I belonged there. Selina and Grace had noticed that too, and they were hopping mad.

Jack introduced me to everyone, but I only took in a very few details. I already knew Jenny and Charles. She looked at my outfit, smiled and winked, then glanced at Selina, who was controlling her annoyance using the same methods as Grace earlier. Grace's mouth was shut like a trap, and she glared.

So I knew I was doing exactly what Jack wanted.

He introduced me to a young man called Derek Lamming, who sat with Selina, his arm on the back of her chair, continually casting her nervous glances. I think he was really glad to see me. Then there was Harry Oxton, who looked about sixty, and hovered over Grace as Derek did Selina.

Among the others the one who stood out was Raymond Keller, nice-looking, early forties, who seemed genuinely friendly with Jack. The rest were just names and faces in a blur.

Jack's explanation of my presence was a

masterpiece. He had hoped to invite me for the cruise, but I had already been committed to visit various friends in Europe. However, several crises had erupted, forcing me to flee with little more than what I was wearing. Luckily he had been around to scoop me up and bring me on board for the rest of the trip.

I was awed. I tell a good tale myself, when it's necessary, but this man had the right touch to make it convincing. It made me wonder just what did go on in the boardroom when he was in charge. Not bullying. I was sure of that. He'd get his own way by talking the hind legs off a donkey.

Grace asked me some pretty barbed questions, but I was getting comfortably into the part now, and managed to parry them. I have to admit, too, that Jack helped me.

'Don't worry the poor girl, now, Grace. She's starving. All she wants is to feed her face, then go out on a huge shopping spree to replace her wardrobe. Hurry up, Della. My credit cards are itching for some exercise.'

Those were words I loved to hear.

He then got a bit high and mighty, urging me away from the table before I was ready. I complained about it when we got into the motor boat.

'Strategy,' he assured me. 'I had the boat

ready and I got you into it before Grace could think up an excuse to come with us.'

There was a taxi waiting for us on the quay. More strategy. Before I knew it we were being whisked up the hill to the streets of Monte Carlo, where the luxury shops congregated.

Ever been let loose in Aladdin's cave and told to do your worst? I made the most of it because I wanted to buy as much as possible before I woke up. Even if it wasn't a dream, I knew it would never happen again.

The first shop was smart casuals, and I was dizzy after the first glance. Jack murmured in my ear, 'Are you ready?'

'Yes.'

'Steady?'

'Yes.'

'OK. *Spend money.*'

So I did. After all, he was my employer, and I had to take his orders. And if there's one thing I know how to do, it's spend money.

'Just what kind of personality am I supposed to have?' I asked him at one point. 'Am I sporty, slinky, a creature of the sun or of the night?'

'All those,' he said. 'Shirts and trousers, clinging gowns—short and long—bikinis— whatever. We've got to cover this from every angle.'

Choosing clothes with him was fun, because *he* found it fun. He watched for ages while I paraded for him, with never a sign of boredom.

After the casual shop we went to another one for dresses. Then another shop for lingerie, another for shoes, and far, far more of everything than I could possibly need for this trip.

'How long are we going to be on the boat?' I asked as he signed things.

'As long as I can make it last,' he said, finishing with a flourish.

'But it can't be more than a few days, can it?'

'Trying to escape me already?' he asked, with a grin that made him gorgeous.

'No way! It's just that you're buying me more than I'll need.'

'Of course,' he said, slightly shocked. 'We can't be economical. Think of my reputation. When parcels start arriving on *The Hawk* everyone must be able to see that you have ten times what you actually need. And another thing,' he added, trying to look stern, 'I expect you to do a lot of sunbathing by the pool. If I see you in the same bikini twice, you're in dead trouble, lady.'

I liked this man.

He told the shops to deliver everything to *The Hawk* at once.

'All except this,' he said, indicating the very smart blue dress I was wearing. 'It's just right for lunching at the Hotel de Paris.'

'You can't get into that restaurant without a reservation,' I warned him.

It was a slip, but he didn't seem to notice.

'I have a reservation,' he said. 'I called them before we left the boat.'

Of course. I should have known that he would have done.

So we went there and had lunch high up, looking down at Monte Carlo. I could just make out *The Hawk* and something else that didn't please me at all.

'*The Silverado* is still there,' I said in disgust.

'Forget Vanner. I won't let him get to you.'

Who cared about Vanner anyway? Who cared about anything except the grilled turbot they were serving and the perfect wine? And the man sitting opposite me. Who cared about anything but him?

He was looking at me with one raised eyebrow.

'Tell me something,' he said. 'Why were you working for Vanner? I don't suppose he paid more than peanuts, and he didn't treat you well. You must have been desperate.'

'I do freelance work in department stores,

demonstrating goods,' I said, sticking to the truth as far as possible. 'A job fell through and I took the first thing that was offered—being a waitress on *The Silverado*. There wasn't time to check it out. When I realised how much more than a waitress I was supposed to be, we were already out at sea.'

'And that's the whole story?'

'What else could there be?'

'I suppose you could tell me how come a young woman who knows so much about good living needs to work as a demonstrator or a waitress.'

'You don't know how much I know,' I said uneasily.

'I've watched you choosing good clothes like an expert. You're used to money, and you're familiar with Monte Carlo—otherwise you'd never have known that you need a reservation for this place.'

So he had noticed my slip after all!

'All right, all right,' I said. 'Daddy was a millionaire, and I was brought up in the lap of luxury. But we fell on hard times.'

He surveyed my wryly. 'So you're not going to reveal anything?'

'Nope. I told you, the less you know about me the better. I have no past, no life outside this moment.'

'Well, you can't blame me for trying to guess.'

'Don't waste the effort. Whatever you're thinking about me is wrong.'

'You don't know what I'm thinking about you.'

'Maybe not. But whatever it is, it's wrong. I'm not like—what you think.'

'I think you're one crazy lady.'

'OK, you've got that bit right,' I conceded.

'And I'll get the rest right too,' he said in a teasing voice. 'Because I want to know all about you. And I'm going to.'

I shrugged. 'If you think you can.'

Inside, I was vowing that there were things about my life that he would never know—not if I could prevent it.

'Woman of mystery, eh?'

'The less *you* can find out, the less others can find out,' I said. 'And that's how you need it. Now, why don't you tell me about myself? My official self, that is. What's our story?'

His eyes gleamed. 'It's no use changing the subject.'

'Yes, it is,' I said at once. 'Changing the subject is the best diversionary tactic ever created, and, considering how often you've used it yourself, you must know that.'

'How do you know I use it myself?'

'Because you're up to every trick.'

'How do you know I'm up to every trick?'

'Are you saying that Bully Jack isn't?'

'Will you leave Bully Jack out of this? He doesn't exist. He's a fantasy figure that the PR boys have invented. He's good for the company image, but that's all.'

'Do you mean,' I asked indignantly, 'that you don't crush everyone beneath your feet? That you don't smash rivals with a ruthless mailed fist?'

He made a wry, apologetic face. 'Sorry.'

'Well, I was never so disappointed!'

He smiled and I caught my breath.

'Are you really?' he said.

And suddenly I didn't know what to say.

CHAPTER FIVE

Della's story

SUDDENLY one corner of Jack's mouth quirked in a crooked smile.

'What?' I challenged.

'Do you realise we've known each other less than twenty-four hours?'

'I don't believe it. But, yes, it's true. It was only last night that we met, outside the casino. What were you doing there all alone?'

'Escaping. We'd all been out together, but I wanted some time to myself. So I changed my cufflinks and got away while they weren't looking.'

'You changed your cufflinks?' I echoed, wondering if I'd heard right.

'Sure. You noticed them, remember? You said the silver plate was wearing off.'

'Well, they looked really odd—so cheap and tacky.'

'That's why I wore them. They belonged to Grandpa Nick, and he always swore that they brought him luck. I suppose they did, in a kind of way. He started the family firm.'

'He founded the great Bullen empire?'

'Lord, no! He wasn't into founding empires. He enjoyed laughing too much. He was a wicked old so-and-so.'

He gave a reminiscent grin that said everything about his love for his grandfather. It made me like him enormously. And when I say like I mean like. This was nothing to do with the sensations that had been giving me such a hard time almost since the very moment I'd met Jack. It was a warm, friendly feeling, as if I really knew him and we were part of the same family.

And in a sense we were—the family of people who adored their grandfathers—because I felt the same about mine.

'All he had was a small grocery shop,' Jack resumed. 'My father went to work for him and then shunted him aside. Grandpa went into early retirement and, since my mother was dead, I got to spend a lot of time with him. He became my favourite person, and I think I was his, even more than his son. He admired my father's abilities, but he was scared of him. I was a bit nervous myself.'

He fell silent while the waiter brought the

next course and the next wine. When we were alone again I said, 'Go on. Don't stop there.'

'Grandpa Nick and I were like a couple of kids, fooling around together. He never really grew up. I wish I could describe him properly.'

'You don't need to,' I said. 'He sounds exactly like mine.'

'Really? Tell me about him?'

'He's never grown up either. Just like you said. Grandad has a child's ability to see the world as he wants it to be, and he's a great spinner of tales. When I was a little girl I thought it was wonderful, having someone who could dress the whole world up in glitter. I was furious when I discovered that other people call it lying, because it isn't. It's just fantasising, and when you're used to it, it's easy to sort out the truth.'

'What did your parents say about his fantasies?'

'I barely remember them. They died when I was two, and Grandad raised me.'

'All alone? I mean, you didn't have a grandmother?'

'No, she was dead too. It was just him and me.'

I laughed suddenly, because things were coming back to me. Nice things that made me happy to remember.

'This is what I mean about his stories. According to Grandad, a posse of social workers descended on him, trying to wrench me from his arms, and he beat them off at the door. Actually, his sister told me that he was visited by one friendly, understanding social worker, who had far too much on her plate and was relieved to mark this case "Solved". When Grandad told her he could manage perfectly well she couldn't get out of there fast enough.'

'Did you have many other relatives?'

'Loads. I was too young to realise why my parents had vanished, and I remember the family getting together a lot, and people crying. Grandad cried more than anyone, but he also cuddled me. Sometimes he cuddled and cried at the same time. We had a wonderful life together. We loved each other and we laughed a lot, and we were happy.'

I stopped because I was suddenly flooded with emotion as I thought of Grandad, how much I loved him and how wretched he was right now. It seemed terrible to be sitting here enjoying the high life while he—

'What is it?' Jack asked me.

'Nothing,' I said hastily.

'You're crying.'

'I'm not.'

I knew he wasn't fooled, but mercifully he

didn't press it. His manner simply became more gentle.

'You love him very much, don't you?' he asked.

'Yes,' I said, blowing my nose. 'You said you and Grandpa Nick were like a couple of kids, and that's how it is with Grandad and me. He looks after me, I look after him.'

'And it's been that way for a long time, hasn't it?' he asked. 'Since you were—what? Ten?'

'More like six,' I said.

'Me too. I can't claim as young as six, but I can remember helping Nick out with the books at the store, because he'd promised Dad he'd have them done by next day and he hadn't even started them. He kept putting them off because he was hopeless at figures. I could manage figures OK. I don't mean I was brilliant, but my mind worked that way. His didn't. He thought it was rocket science. So I did the books, which didn't leave me any time for my homework. So he came up to the school next day and gave them a sob story to get me off. I didn't know where to look. I was so sure they'd see through him. But they didn't. He did it so well.'

'Oh, yes,' I said, remembering my childhood. 'He did it well.'

Now I really liked Jack. Having daft grandfathers, so alike that they might have been twins, was a true bond.

'Nick was full of silly jokes and superstitions,' Jack resumed. 'He believed in lucky charms, and he had a dozen of them, all supposed to work for something different. The most important were the cufflinks. He was wearing them when he proposed to the most wonderful woman in the world, even though he reckoned he had no chance. But he was wrong. She said yes. So he decided they must be lucky, and he treasured them always. It meant a lot that he gave them to me. We both knew Dad wouldn't have understood.'

'Do they work?' I asked.

'Often enough to be hair-raising. Last night I went to the casino twice, the first time wearing a pair of my own.'

'Solid gold?'

'Please!' he said in a scandalised voice. 'Bully Jack doesn't waste his time on gold. Solid platinum.'

I nodded sagely. 'Twice the price.'

'Right. Anyway I lost, which is what you expect in a casino. Then later I went back a second time, I was wearing Nick's ''lucky'' links, and won ten grand.'

'Aha! That's how come you can afford me!'

He surveyed me wryly. 'We passed ten

grand about eleven-thirty this morning. And we haven't even started on jewellery yet.'

'Your grandpa sounds great. I can understand why you liked him so much.'

'I loved him. Mind you, I blame him for everything. If he hadn't started that store my Dad couldn't have built it up into a chain and then left the lot to me. It was made very clear that I had to become a tycoon—whether I wanted it or not.'

'And you expect me to believe that you didn't?'

'I wanted to be a vet. But the trouble with money is that if you have it you find that more keeps sticking to you, like mud. And people depend on you—the workforce, shareholders, your sister. You dream about getting out from under, but how can you when it's going to affect them?'

'I suppose we all dream of getting out from under,' I mused. 'What would your version be? Becoming a vet at last?'

'No, it's too late for that. I'd just like to get away and be a hobo of the waterways. I'd have a barge, and a great, stupid dog. Or maybe I'd be really extravagant and have two.'

'Just you and the dogs?'

'Probably. There aren't too many people you could ask to spend their lives like that.'

'Oh, this is to be a lifetime thing?'

'You bet. The whole point is to be completely free of all the heavy stuff—obligations, responsibilities, and above all people's expectations.'

I'm not sure if he knew it, but he gave a little sigh as he said the last words, and it told me a great deal.

'That's where the shoe really pinches?'

'And how!' he said with feeling.

'Hence the dog?'

'Dogs. At least three. I've just decided. Dogs have the right idea. They don't expect anything from you except love and care. They aren't trying to talk you into a bad investment, or get you drunk, hoping to muddle you into something you'll regret. They don't pay you daft compliments in an attempt to seduce you, because you're rich and they want to get their hands on the goodies. And above all they aren't trying to badger you into a marriage that would suit them.'

His voice got a little ragged on the last words.

'Are you really that modest?' I asked. 'Or is it false modesty?'

'What is?'

'Your assumption that the women who seduce you are only after your money.'

Personally, I could think of a million other good reasons. Well, one anyway.

'I only said they *try* to seduce me,' he pointed out.

'Of course. And you say, "Get thee behind me, Satan." '

'Never mind that,' he said hastily. 'We've got distracted. And I'd like to make it clear that when I mentioned money I wasn't accusing you. If there's one lady in the world who isn't trying to fleece me, it's you.'

'Well, I don't have to fleece you, do I?' I pointed out. 'You're spending a fortune on me without giving me the trouble of seducing you—always assuming that I could.'

'I'm not answering that. You don't *need* me to answer that.'

I just smiled.

'And,' he pointed out, 'always assuming that you'd want to.'

'And *I'm* not answering *that*,' I told him. 'You think I came down in the last shower?'

'I guess neither of us did,' he replied, with meaning.

After that we fell silent for a while, both of us thinking over what we'd just said, what we'd left unsaid, and what we both understood.

'I'm only saying,' I resumed at last, 'that I

could be all kinds of gold-digger, just biding my time, waiting to ask for more.'

'And last night? Covering me with bruises?'

'I didn't know who you were.'

'A true gold-digger *would* have known who I was. You have no idea about these women, Della. They have filing systems, filled with photographs of men, plus full details of every penny they possess. They know more about my assets than I do. And you're not like that. I know you.'

'You don't know me.'

'I do.'

'Don't.'

'Do.'

The waiter appeared again and we fell silent, trying not to laugh.

When the soufflé had been served, with a different wine, he returned to the subject.

'If I assume most women are fortune hunters it's because those are the kind I tend to meet. Maybe some of them aren't, but it gets hard to tell the difference. Women have come to feel almost unreal to me. In fact, so do most things.'

I sipped from my glass, and the wine felt like heaven. Seeing the look on my face, he refilled the glass.

'Of course,' he added, a tad too casually, 'there is one thing that could give me cause for suspicion about you, and that's the fact that you're so secretive about yourself. Now if you could just come up with a few personal details I could stop worrying...'

'Too late!' I told him, laughing. 'You should have played that card about five minutes ago. You've missed the trick now.'

'I was afraid of that,' he said. 'If this were a boardroom I'd have known exactly when to play it. But sitting here with you, like this— I'm confused.'

'Good,' I told him. 'I prefer that.'

'I'm not going to win a single round with you, am I?'

I shook my head.

'I know it's hard to believe—' he sighed '—but when I'm out of the boardroom all my confidence deserts me, and then I need help.'

He gave me a pathetic smile that would have knocked me out if I hadn't been getting thoroughly suspicious.

I'll be honest. It knocked me out anyway. This man could get to you even when you knew he was up to every trick.

'Don't—you—dare,' I breathed slowly. 'Don't you dare sit there and play for sympathy. Do I look stupid?'

'You look good enough to eat,' he said shamelessly.

'I'm warning you, Jack. Do not ask me to feel sorry for you. And take that penitent look off your face, because that doesn't fool me either.'

He gave his brilliant grin.

'It was worth a try,' he said. 'But perhaps I should have known better. You see through me. That's the nicest thing about you.' He added in a considering tone, 'Well—almost the nicest.'

He waited for me to pick up on his last words. Our eyes met—his querying, mine telling him he could wait for ever. He backed down first.

'Touché,' he said, raising his glass to me.

We understood each other perfectly.

'Tell me about Bully Jack,' I said.

He groaned. 'Not you too. I told you, he's an invention. He gives my PR department something to do, and that's about all. OK, a reputation for ruthlessness can sometimes be useful. And Grace fosters it. She has actually given newspaper interviews, painting Bully Jack in lurid colours.'

'Why does Grace have such a hold over you?'

'Because she looked after me when our father died. I was fifteen. He did a very unfair thing, leaving me everything and her nothing. I put it right as soon as I could, so justice has been done if we're only talking about money. But I've swallowed up her life, and it's a bit late for her to reclaim it now.'

'But you must be in your thirties,' I protested. 'So she could have reclaimed her life at least ten years ago.'

'Well,' he said vaguely, 'she felt she should go on looking after me. And of course I'm grateful.'

In my opinion Grace had become domineering and power-hungry, playing on his feelings of guilt. I didn't think he'd swallowed up her life, but I could see her swallowing his.

I didn't say so, because I could see that this was something he was unwilling to confront. He had a kind heart, and it undermined his attempts to break free.

Over coffee he became businesslike, outlining the salary he intended to pay me. When I protested that it was too much he said briskly, 'That's enough out of you. Drink up. We still have jewellery to buy.'

He considered me like a film director planning a shot.

'You're going to be a challenge. The gamine look isn't easy to adorn. Trying to put a tiara on hair as short as yours can be the very devil. Luckily you have a nice long neck, so we can hang some long earrings on you.'

'I don't like long earrings,' I said defiantly.

'You'll do as you're told,' he told me, with his nicest grin—i.e. his wickedest. There was no difference.

'Oh, will I?'

'Yes, you will. You see, I'm going to be a tyrant—no, don't giggle. It's time you found out what a tyrant I am. So if I want you in long diamond earrings, you'll wear them. The same applies to pearls, emeralds, sapphires, rubies—'

'Rubies don't suit me.'

'Don't interrupt. Really top class rubies suit everyone. If you think otherwise you've been accepting them from the wrong men—cheapskates who didn't get you the best.'

He left the question hanging in the air. I refused to answer, other than to say, 'Is that so?'

'That's so.'

'I must send them a memo,' I said lightly.

'Do. And while you're at it tell them that you're mine now, so they can just stop thinking about you.'

'I never let any man stop thinking about me,' I said firmly. 'After all, why should they?'

'No reason at all that I can think of,' he said, in a voice that was suddenly soft and vibrant.

Shivers went through me at that sound. I waited, hoping he would pursue the subject. When he didn't I tossed an ember on the fire.

'Anyway, you know nothing at all about my friends or what they think of,' I said lightly.

His eyes met mine, teasing, challenging.

'You know as well as I do what every man who sees you thinks of,' he said with meaning.

That morning in the great bed, his naked body touching mine, responding to me, making me respond to him against my will, the sight of him dashing across the carpet to the bathroom in all his glory. Everything came back to me in a moment, making me warm all over with intense delight.

'I know what they think of, and I know what I think of,' I said with a shrug. 'They're not necessarily the same thing.'

'Well, it's time for you to turn your attention to this afternoon's purchases,' he said, using the voice of a man forcing himself back to normal. 'It's not just jewellery, but anything else you can think of. What? What is it?'

I'd burst out laughing.

'You should keep your voice down. Do you realise how many people heard you say that? You know what they'll think?'

'They'll think I'm crazy about you,' he said, smiling.

'No, they won't. They'll think I'm your tart, your bit on the side, your kept woman.'

'You sound as though you'd enjoy that.'

'In reality I probably wouldn't, but I've always had this fantasy of being a world-class courtesan—maybe Madame de Pompadour, or another of those *grande horizontales*. Great fun. Well, fun for about five minutes. Then desperately boring.'

'But surely Madame de Pompadour did more than lie around looking good? She had a terrific brain and helped the French king run the country. I see you as being like that.'

'You're right. I could never resist the temptation to stick my oar in.'

He grinned. 'I've been warned. Now, let's go and see if I can distract your attention with a few baubles.'

He took me into a succession of jewellery shops. At his command they laid everything out for my inspection, and I held my breath at the beauty of it all.

He wouldn't tell me the prices, but I could see they were all fabulous. Earrings, bracelets, necklaces—in all stones, but mostly in diamonds. Until that moment I hadn't known how madly I loved diamonds.

'But it's all too much,' I protested in an undervoice.

'Not if you're going to make the impression I want. They'll be watching.'

I couldn't argue with that, so I just had to

put up with him showering me with a fortune. It was hard, but I gritted my teeth and did my duty.

'We'll be the talk of Monte Carlo after this,' I said, while the assistants in the last shop were packing things up.

'Monte Carlo?' He looked shocked. 'Europe.'

'The world,' I declared triumphantly.

And then I saw it. A tiny diamond brooch in the shape of a penguin. I guessed the price was a fraction of anything else in the shop, but it was charming and exquisite and I fell in love with it.

Jack saw me gazing at it.

'That?' he asked.

I nodded, explaining, 'I'm mad about penguins.'

He wasn't like other men. He didn't say something crass like, *What about all that pricey stuff I've bought you?* He understood at once, and pinned the brooch onto me.

'You're right,' he said. 'It looks perfect on you.'

When it was time to leave Jack was carrying so much valuable jewellery that the shop provided its own armoured car to take us down to the quay. A phone call ensured that the motor boat would be waiting.

There were several faces leaning over the rail when we reached *The Hawk*. Jenny and Charles were there, frankly agog. Jenny told me later that they'd seen the parcels arrive earlier and everyone had been riveted by the sight. Except for Grace and Selina, who had ostentatiously *not* been riveted.

'Can I come and see?' Jenny asked eagerly.

She came down to the cabin with me, while Jack fled to the sanctuary of the bar with Charles and several of the other men.

'Good, that's got rid of them,' Jenny said gleefully. 'Now we can have some fun.'

While I was showing her my new clothes she ordered champagne by phone, and we drank it together.

'I've been keeping an eye on Selina for you.' She chuckled. 'She's seen the writing on the wall and she's mad as fire.'

'Is she in love with him?' I asked.

'No way. He's just the best catch around. Don't worry, you're not breaking her heart. She'll probably end up marrying Derek, who's nutty about her, and has almost as big a bank balance as she needs.'

'Is she really as bad as that?'

'Worse. She used to date Charles, but his firm had a crash and he lost a lot of money.

She dropped him just like that. Luckily I came along and distracted him.'

She gave a smile that told a lot about her marriage. Then abruptly the smiled faded and she yelped, *'That!'*

I'd appeared in a long, black velvet dress, low in the front and even lower at the back.

'Wear that one,' she said. 'It's sensational. And diamonds. Do you have any?'

'I don't think there's a diamond left in the world.'

We had a great time dressing me to kill, and Jenny's instinct was spot on. Black velvet and diamonds were a great combination.

'Can I come in?' That was Jack, calling from outside the door.

'Come in,' I called back.

He walked in and stood stock still, gazing at me in a way that filled me with satisfaction.

'Will she do?' Jenny carolled. 'Will she do or won't she do?'

'She'll do,' Jack said quietly.

That was all. But I'd seen the way he looked at me, and it said, *Tonight.*

Jack had come to tell us that he was taking everyone to dinner ashore that evening. It turned out to be a shrewd idea. There were too many of us for one table, so we were split among three, and he managed to keep me away from Selina and Grace. I found myself sitting with Jack on one side and Raymond Keller on the other.

Raymond seemed a nice guy, apart from a tendency to look down my dress, but since it was designed for that I supposed it wasn't fair to blame him.

Charles and Jenny were facing me, and the others were youngish couples. They weren't trying to trap Jack for themselves or their daughters, so the atmosphere was pleasant. I began to understand that Jack was a master of tactics.

He played up, slipping his arm around my shoulders whenever he wasn't eating, clinking wine glasses with me, and sometimes murmuring in my ear.

I could just see Grace and Selina, who kept turning their heads to send forked lightning at me. I reckoned they were calculating every penny of the diamonds' worth, and if they could have killed me, they would have done.

'Now you've had a chance to relax with some of them,' Jack said to me in the taxi. 'But tomorrow you'll be right in the lions' den.'

'Just lead me to it.'

'You were a knockout tonight. Just keep doing it.'

'Doing what, precisely?' I teased.

He drew a ragged breath. 'Whatever it is you're doing. And please don't laugh like that. It makes my life extremely difficult.'

I laughed again. I wanted his life to be difficult.

When we were on board we said goodnight to everyone and went straight to the cabin.

I ran a hot bath and snuggled down blissfully into the suds, thinking of the night to come. I told myself that I couldn't be sure what was going to happen, but I'd chosen my nightdress very carefully.

Nothing blatant, and not as sexy as Jenny's, but silky and elegant. And it wasn't going to hide a lot from a man in the same bed.

During the day we'd talked with a sensual undertone. Whatever the subject, we'd actually been speaking about something else that didn't need any words.

We'd undressed each other with our eyes and our minds, and that had been very nice. But I knew that I'd really decided *Yes!* when we'd swapped grandfather stories. That was when my heart had warmed to him as much as my body.

Now I was preparing to make love to a man I'd known barely twenty-four hours—something I'd never done before. And why? Because he loved his grandfather. Put like that, it made no sense. Except to me.

I towelled myself dry and used a few discreet dabs of perfume. Then I slipped on the beautiful pale blue nightdress, and I was all ready. Taking a deep breath, I went back to the bedroom.

There was only one small bedside lamp on. In the shadows I could discern that the other side of the bed, which had been empty when I went into the bathroom, now had a bump. A bump that lay with its back to me, breathing evenly.

Next to it was another bump, the shape of a pillow.

I wanted to scream and shout. I wanted to thump him and say how dared he go to sleep? I wanted to throw every piece of glass across the room until it smashed to fragments.

But I didn't, of course.

Instead I climbed into my side of the bed, put out the light and lay in the darkness, silently reciting all the rudest words I knew.

CHAPTER SIX

Della's Story

Next day we left Monte Carlo and headed for Sardinia. It was time for me to do my stuff.

I made a grand entrance, sauntering to the smaller of the two swimming pools, where most of the others were stretched out. When their eyes were on me I pulled off a floaty chiffon jacket, leaving nothing but a tiny pink bikini. Then I stretched out and closed my eyes, as if totally unaware of everyone.

'Well done,' said Jack, stretching out beside me.

I was lying on my back, my eyes closed. Now I opened them halfway and surveyed him. I managed a smile, but in truth I was furious with him for last night. To compound his crimes he was wearing tiny swimming trunks that cleared up the question of his shape once and for all.

His build was slightly heavy, but he was tall with no fat, and gave an impression of controlled physical power that his elegant suits normally concealed. Seeing him almost naked reminded me of what might have been mine, and hadn't been, and it didn't improve my mood.

'Good morning,' I murmured. 'Have we met?'

'Yes, I'm the fellow who brought your coffee this morning. And I didn't even get a tip.'

'I never tip the hired help,' I murmured languidly.

He laughed, and whispered, 'That's great. Play the indifferent card for all it's worth. Act like I'm dirt beneath your feet.'

If he'd known how much I'd have liked to do just that he wouldn't have risked saying it.

'Are they watching us?' I murmured.

'And how!'

'In that case—'

I brushed the backs of my fingers against his face. At once he took my hand, turned it over and kissed the palm. I braced myself against the tremors that went through me, and managed to smile.

'I've brought you some sunscreen,' he said. 'You shouldn't lie out like this with that fair skin.'

He handed me the bottle and I rubbed the

lotion in well, until Jack took it and said, 'Turn over.'

He did my back and my hips, down as far as the bikini bottom. Then I felt him undo the clasp of the bikini top and begin to work cream into my skin there.

'I had to undo it or you'd have had a mark,' he explained.

It would have been the easiest thing in the world to let his hand drift down the sides a little. But he didn't. He simply finished oiling me and fastened the clasp again. It was like being guarded by a Boy Scout.

After a while someone called him from further down the pool and he went to talk to them. I stayed where I was, controlling my feelings with an effort. How I'd have loved to toss him into his own pool and hold him under. But the sun was making me sleepy, so I decided to let him live—for now.

I must have sort of dozed, because the next thing I was aware of was a hand rubbing more lotion into my back.

'Mmm!' I said.

'Like it?' asked a laughing voice.

That wasn't Jack. I twisted around and found myself looking at Raymond Keller.

He was a pleasant sight—fortyish, lean and

strongly built, with reddish hair. I was still sufficiently irked with Jack to do a little flirting.

'I'm not quite sure,' I mused.

'Well, let me do a little more so that you can decide.'

'No, I think that's enough for today,' I said, sitting up and regarding him.

'You know,' he said, 'I've been trying to think where I've seen you before.'

'Maybe you haven't.'

'Sure I have. You definitely look familiar.'

'You're probably just confusing me with some other girl in a pink bikini.'

'It's not really pink,' he said. 'More a kind of flesh colour. From a distance you look as if you're not wearing anything. I've been watching you and studying the matter very seriously.'

His grin made it impossible to be offended. Just the same, I played it safe.

'It's pink,' I said decidedly. 'It makes us all look alike, you know.'

'Not you. You don't look like any other girl. Wait! I've got it! You were at the Davisons' château last summer. We danced the night away, but you never told me your name.'

I made a pretence of considering this. 'I'm afraid I don't remember.'

He reeled off some more names and places, while I fenced and parried. It meant nothing.

He knew we hadn't met before. This was just a traditional opening gambit.

But then I struck lucky.

Jack returned and sat down on my other side, greeting Raymond briefly.

'Della and I have just been trying to remember where we first met,' Raymond said.

'Really?' Jack said politely. 'Have you come up with anything?'

'I'm not sure. I sure don't seem to have made much of an impression on her if we did. How about the theatre, Della? I go to a lot of opening nights. Maybe I saw you at the opening of *Flowers in the Rain*?'

'Do you mean that dreadful evening when they had to stop the show because a woman in the front row was taken ill?' I asked.

'That's right,' he said, beaming.

'The actor playing the lead was put right off his stride,' I said, in the voice of someone remembering. 'He never really recovered after that—kept stumbling over his lines.'

'Fancy us both being there! Yes, you definitely smiled at me in the Circle Bar.'

'It's a small world,' Jack observed.

For some reason Raymond didn't stick around now Jack was there, and when some of the other men dived into the pool he joined them.

'What was all that about?' Jack asked me. 'Did you really see him at that first night?'

'No, I wasn't even there. I heard about it from someone who was. The point is, he's now convinced he's seen me around, and will vouch for me as one of his own circle. By the time he talks to Grace and Selina we'll have been at school together.'

Jack roared with laughter.

'You're a really tricky lady,' he said.

I'd only meant it as a joke, but I spoke truer than I knew—because suddenly Grace and Selina began to eye me more cautiously. They just weren't sure any more, and that suited me fine. It suited Jack too. He was loving every moment.

There was a bar at the side of the pool, with stools just below the water line. After a quick dip, I swam over to get a long orange juice, and while I was sitting there, sipping, Selina came and joined me.

I have to admit she had a figure to be proud of. She was statuesque, and might run to fat later, but just now she was at her best—as her black bikini revealed.

Her manner was almost friendly.

'So you're an old friend of Raymond's,' she said. 'You should have told us.'

'I didn't get the chance,' I said. 'Since I arrived things have just happened, one on top of the other. No time to think, really.'

I simpered, just in case she didn't know what I meant by 'no time to think'.

She managed to maintain her smile.

'And I don't really know Raymond,' I continued. 'Just distantly.'

'Jack must have been incredibly surprised by you turning up so suddenly?'

'We-ell, between you and me, I don't think he was as surprised as all that.' I became confiding. 'You know Jack. You can never really tell what he's about to do next. Well, I'm exactly the same. Like calling to like, I guess.'

'I wouldn't have called Jack unpredictable,' she said, in a slightly tense voice. 'His firm has been built on steadiness and reliability.'

I shrugged in a feather-headed sort of way. 'Oh, business!'

'Business is important,' she said smugly. 'Of course if you can't share his interests—'

'I do share his interests. Just not about business!'

I said this with my most wide-eyed gaze, and threw in a titter for good measure.

There was a time when I'd wanted be an actress. How I didn't make it, I'll never understand.

'What are you two doing with your heads

together?' came Jack's voice from the water behind us. 'Are all the men being torn apart? Tell.'

'Why do men always think we have nothing else to talk about but them?' I asked. 'We weren't even thinking about you. Go away.'

'Come in and swim with me,' he said. 'The water's fantastic.'

Selina immediately slipped off her stool and swam towards him, leaving him no choice but to look pleased and glide away with her.

I wasn't alone for long. Derek Lamming immediately took her place on one side, and Selina's father popped up on the other. After a while they were joined by Raymond. Even Harry Oxton swam over and took a stool. He was Grace's beau, according to Jack, and from the way her mouth tightened I guess she felt a bit proprietorial.

So there I was, surrounded by men and flirting like mad—especially with Derek and Harry. I don't know how long this went on, but it ended abruptly with me being yanked off my stool from behind. The next moment I was underwater, with Jack's arm about my waist.

'What are you playing at?' he asked me as our heads broke water.

'I'm trying to do a really good job for you,' I said.

'Giving Derek and poor old Harry the glad eye?'

'Of course. It'll warn Selina and Grace not to take them for granted. Look, Selina's already reclaiming her property.'

Sure enough, Selina had taken my vacated stool and was smiling at Derek.

'You're wicked,' Jack told me.

'No, just a good employee who thinks of everything.'

'Hmm. You seem to have forgotten that you're supposed to be mad about me. Now you've made eyes at the others, when is it my turn?'

He still had his arms about me, holding me close in the water. I had one arm round his neck and was looking up at him.

'But I *am* making eyes at you,' I said.

'And that's all I get?'

This was becoming dangerous. I could see us heading up the same cul-de-sac as before. But duty must come first, so I slipped a hand around the back of his head and drew it down to me.

His mouth seemed to fit so naturally over mine, and everything was easy. I tried to remember that we were performing for spectators, but there was a thin line between that and burning up, and we'd crossed it the first evening.

Even treading water, he knew just how to tease and incite, so that I found myself doing the same to him, using skills that I hadn't known I possessed. Perhaps nobody had inspired me to use them before.

I felt his tongue against my lips—not commanding, just suggesting, retreating, returning. He was clever. He didn't give me time to make up my mind before he'd moved on to my neck, just below the ear. Some devil must have told him about that place, because it's just where I like to be kissed.

I ran my hands over the heavy muscles of his neck, his shoulders, then into his hair, and through the contact of our skin I could feel him almost losing control. But not quite.

Then I forgot everything else, including treading water. The same must have happened to Jack, because gradually we slid under the surface.

It didn't make any difference, because by then we weren't breathing anyway. We actually ran out of air before we discovered where we were, and had to shoot up to the surface, gasping and spluttering.

Charles and Jenny applauded. 'We were taking bets on how long you'd be down there,' Charles called.

Jack's eyes met mine, and we knew we'd made the same decision. In a moment we'd vanished below the water again, making it last as long as possible. We were laughing when we came up.

It was a good way to live if you didn't let yourself think of anything else. So I decided to go with it and have fun.

We spent that night at sea. One of the staff doubled as a DJ, so there was going to be a dance when dinner was over. I'd already developed a light tan, so I wore a long white dress to show it off and Jack nodded approval.

The last thing I did was take out my little diamond penguin. I've always been crazy about penguins, and whoever had designed this brooch had managed to catch their quirky daftness.

'I'm going to wear Charlie,' I told Jack, holding up the brooch.

That startled him. 'You call a brooch Charlie?'

'No, the penguin's called Charlie.'

He grinned. 'If you say so.'

'I love him to bits. Can you pin him on for me? Careful!'

He'd dropped Charlie and slightly lost his

balance at the same time. When he retrieved the brooch from the carpet the pin was slightly bent, where it had been trodden on.

'Oh, no!' I said in dismay. 'Does that mean it's unwearable?'

'No, I think I can do it,' Jack said, squeezing hard.

Luckily he had strong fingers, and the metal was soon almost right, with just a tiny kink left to show that anything had happened.

He pinned it onto my left shoulder and smiled at the effect.

'Charlie,' he said. 'Fancy calling a penguin Charlie!'

'He's my penguin; I'll call him what I like.'

He kissed the end of my nose. 'Whatever you want. You look fantastic, and you're doing a great job. But if Raymond or the others want to dance with you—'

'I'll dance with them,' I said.

I'm not sure that was the answer he wanted.

'As long as you know that you don't have to,' he said at last. 'You do what you feel like. Nothing else. There's no need to put up with any funny business. This isn't *The Silverado*.'

'I know,' I said, warmed by his considera-tion. 'But I should act as if everything is nor-mal, and on a trip like this everyone dances with everyone.'

'They don't give everyone the come-on, as you were in the pool this morning,' he observed, sounding slightly testy.

'But they do. On a cruise there's no other way to pass the time except giving people the come-on.'

'Just don't overdo it,' he said darkly, tucking my hand through his arm. 'Let's go.'

Even Jack had to admit that my methods were effective. Neither Derek nor Harry was allowed near me by their possessive womenfolk. They were in heaven. I don't think either of them had ever received so much attention before.

The one who really hovered over me was Raymond. During a dance he insisted on telling me all about himself—how he expected to take over Consolidated, how much business he and Jack did, how rich he was, how rich he expected to be. I could have sat an exam on Raymond Keller.

The more he talked, the more my brief liking for him faded. Heavens, but he was a bore! Give me Jack any day, with his lightness of touch and refusal to take himself seriously.

When Jack and I were dancing he said, 'Raymond's very taken with you.'

'Don't I know it,' I said grumpily. 'My ears

are aching. Doesn't he ever talk about anyone except himself?'

'I don't think he knows there *is* anyone except himself.'

We laughed together and it was like being back at the Hotel de Paris, when we'd chatted for hours and known each other better in that short time than some people do in a lifetime.

The music was smoochy. He drew me close, so that my head rested on his shoulder, and dropped his own head, turning it slightly into my neck so that his lips brushed my skin.

It was physically exciting, and added to my frustration that I couldn't have him. But it was also strangely cosy. The warmth that swept me was contentment. I could gladly nestle against him like this for ever.

Only it wasn't going to be for ever. Another week. Perhaps less. Already I felt more in tune with him than was wise, but I knew I couldn't be wise. Not with Jack. There was all the rest of my life for wisdom.

And sadness. And loneliness. And being grey and dreary, and knowing that the best and loveliest was behind me.

At last the party broke up and we went down to our cabins.

That kiss in the pool had confirmed something about Jack that I'd started to guess. He was far more complex than he seemed. However it looked, he was always actually in control. Last night had proved it.

Tonight I watched for the ominous signs, determined to get my retaliation in first. The sight of the pillow, firmly placed in the centre of the bed, decided me. I bagged the first bath and emerged yawning.

'I'm so tired,' I said. 'I just want to sleep for an age. Goodnight.'

Not giving him time to say a word, I rolled into bed, pulled the sheet over my head and lay there.

That would show him!

We stopped one night in Cagliari, in southern Sardinia, and explored the old town while the boat took on supplies. I did a bit of shopping with Jenny, who was still watching Jack and me, thrilled by what she took to be our progress.

'I'm so glad he found you,' she said as we sat over coffee. 'I just know you're the one for him.'

'Don't be so sure,' I said, trying to resist the enchanting picture this conjured up.

'You've saved him. But for you, Selina would have had him on toast.'

'I don't think so,' I said, suddenly realising

the truth. 'Jack seems easy-going, but I think he's very stubborn underneath.'

Jenny considered this and nodded. 'Good for you. It takes most people ages to learn that. You really understand him.'

I had to force myself to bring the conversation to an end. I was enjoying it too much.

When we were back on board Jack ceremoniously presented me with a cheque.

'Your first week's pay,' he said. 'And every penny well earned.'

I tucked it away, ready to be cashed as soon as we reached England, thinking how many problems it would solve

After Cagliari, we made a brief stop in Barcelona, then began to head home. A different mood was creeping over everyone. People who had come on the cruise with something in mind began to sense that time was running out. It was now or never. Perhaps that was why Jack kept me closer than ever.

Or perhaps he was keeping an eye on Raymond, who was drinking too much and making a great play of flirting with two women at once. I was never one of them.

There was another dance. I played my part for a while, then slipped away because the atmosphere was stuffy and I needed to breathe. I found a quiet place on deck and stood by the rail, looking out over the water, with the wash stretching away into the darkness.

That would be my life after this, I thought, leading away into a distance that I could not fathom. The only thing I knew for certain was that Jack would not be a part of it. And I knew now that without him it would mean nothing.

'So there you are,' he said, coming up behind me.

'I just came out for some fresh air.'

'Good idea. I'll be glad when we reach Southampton in a few days.'

A few days! Then it would all be over, and he was looking forward to it. But I'd known the terms from the start, and I wasn't going to complain now.

'You're not planning to desert me as soon as we land, I hope,' were his next words. 'We'll have to stay together a while or the others will smell a rat.'

'I can manage a while,' I said, trying not to look too idiotically joyful.

'A few weeks?'

'Yes, probably.'

'But not certainly? Do you have other appointments?'

'You could put it that way,' I said cautiously.

He took my hands. 'We'll get rid of the others and go to my apartment in town. I still officially share a roof with Grace, but I insist on my own place, where I can relax. Your being there will give me the perfect excuse to move in full time.'

So it was still very much a business arrangement. But I was too happy at the reprieve to worry about that. Just a little longer. That was all I asked.

As we began to wander back we heard a shout.

'Hey, Jack! Come and listen to this.'

A group of men were on deck, laughing and cheering over some tipsy joke.

'I'd better go and calm them down,' he said. 'See you later.'

I watched as he joined them, laughing, and gradually drew them inside. I was just thinking of following when a voice in the shadows said, 'I thought I'd never catch you alone.'

It was Raymond Keller. I tried to appear pleasant, but said, 'I was just going in.'

'You can spare me a moment. You'll be glad when you see what I want to give you.'

He'd planted himself in front of me, and before I could protest he opened a box, revealing a really fabulous necklace. Diamonds, of course.

'I've seen how you like diamonds,' he said.

'Raymond, I can't accept these. Please take them away.'

'Oh, come on. I bought them specially for you.'

'You shouldn't have done.'

'Look, you're not going to be with Jack for ever. He's not the faithful type. I don't suppose you are either, but we could have some fun together. How about we leave the ship together—?'

'Get lost,' I said.

'Now, look, I'm making you a fair offer—'

'No, you're making a pest of yourself.'

'You think you can do better than me?'

'I think anyone's better than you. Now, get out of my way.'

'Oh, no, not yet. You've led me on—'

He pounced on me, and there was a short, undignified struggle which ended with me escaping him and holding the box with the necklace over the side.

'Back off,' I said breathlessly, 'or I'll drop it in the water.'

He made a noise between a groan and a shriek. 'You wouldn't do that.'

'I will if you give me any more trouble.'

'What's going on?' It was Jack, who'd heard the noise and come to see what was causing it.

Raymond was beside himself with temper and petulance.

'Your little tart's been leading me on,' he raged.

'If you don't stop saying that I really will drop it in,' I threatened. 'Maybe then you'll believe I'm not interested.'

'You think you've got richer pickings, don't you—?'

That was all Raymond managed to say before Jack floored him.

Raymond sat rubbing his face, more surprised than hurt. Then he leapt up and made for me. I was just drawing my arm back from over the side, but I didn't quite make it. His lunge took me by surprise, and before I could stop it the box was spinning down into the water.

'Serves you right,' Jack said curtly. 'Now, get out of my sight before you follow it.'

Raymond glared, but didn't answer back. He'd seen something in Jack's eyes that made him scuttle away quickly. I'd seen it too, and it startled me. It wasn't the look of a man protecting a business deal. Just what it did mean, I wouldn't let myself speculate. I might get fanciful and think it was jealousy.

He took me in his arms. 'Are you all right?'

'Yes, I'm fine,' I said in a shaking voice.

'Don't cry.'

'I'm not crying. I'm laughing.'

Wave after wave of mirth was welling up inside me. It was terribly funny.

'That necklace,' I said. 'It must have been worth twenty grand. And it all went into the water.'

He began to laugh too. 'That'll teach him better manners next time. How dare he insult you?'

'He's the one who's sorry. I can look after myself.'

'Now she tells me. After I put on that cheesy display of heroics.'

'You're not cheesy,' I assured him.

We went back inside and had another dance, holding each other close so that Raymond would get the point if he happened to be looking. Actually, he wasn't. He'd retired for the night.

But some word must have gone around, because while Jack was fetching me a drink I found myself facing Grace.

'I hope you're proud of yourself,' she said, in a voice like a razorblade. 'It's all due to you that Jack has offended Raymond Keller, and that's a disaster for him.'

'Jack doesn't seem to think so.'

'As though *you'd* know anything about it,' she snapped. 'Keller is going to be the head of one of the biggest firms in the country soon, and that makes him an important man for Jack to know. Why do you think he was invited on this trip?'

'Well, it wasn't for his sparkling conversation, that's for sure,' I retorted.

'It's because he's a man of substance.'

'I know that. He's told me a hundred times, and I'm not interested.'

'Oh, please, don't play the innocent with me. You've been flaunting yourself—turning his head with your cheap fancy-woman tricks, just like you turned Jack's. And what's the result? A brawl. Keller has a black eye, and Jack's lost a useful contact.'

'I'm sorry about that. But I don't see why you blame me.'

'Because a woman like you is always to blame. You've got big ideas, haven't you? Just because Jack's spent a bit of money on you, you think you've got him for life.'

'Is that what I think?'

'Of course it is. I know women of your sort. You think you're entitled to anything you want, but you're just an amusement to Jack. He'll toss you aside when you've served your purpose.'

No matter what, I was determined not to let her make me angry.

'Well, that's his decision,' I said, as coolly as I could manage.

Jack returned with the drinks at that moment. Grace sniffed and flounced off. When Jack asked me what she'd said I passed it off lightly. But I couldn't help worrying in case I'd really damaged him.

CHAPTER SEVEN

Jack's Story

AFTER that misunderstanding with Raymond the party began to break up. We made an un-scheduled stop in Gibraltar because Raymond discovered that urgent business called him home, and Selina's father apparently received a call announcing a crisis in one of his firms. He needed to fly home too, immediately, and Selina and her mother went with him. Derek announced that he would also leave the ship.

Grace said it was all my fault.

'He's seizing his chance to get Selina to him-self,' she snapped. 'They'll be engaged before you're home.'

'I sincerely hope so.'

'Poor Selina has been *disgusted by your be-haviour*,' Grace declared, managing to speak in italics.

I grinned. 'No, she's just realised what a lucky escape she's had. Why don't you write me off as a hopeless case and spend the rest of the trip being nice to Harry?'

Grace sniffed.

I was making plans. After all, Bully Jack was supposed to be the great organiser, the strategic genius who won out by planning everything to the last degree. Let's see if I could do it when it really mattered.

I fixed it so that when we docked in Southampton a fleet of cars would meet the passengers and whisk them back to London—except for me and Della, who would remain onboard for one more night. That way I reckoned we'd have privacy.

Grace didn't like leaving the two of us alone together, but she restricted her comments to, 'Well, I suppose if you're determined to make a fool of yourself—'

'I am,' I assured her. 'Absolutely determined. And I'll tell you something else. I've never enjoyed being a fool so much.'

On the last full day the sun was hot and we all lounged by the pool. Della was the last to arrive, advancing slowly so that everyone could look their fill.

I had to hand it to her. As per my instructions, she wore a different bikini every time, and she did things to a bikini that no other woman had ever done. Her figure was deceptive. While it was covered she looked almost too thin. In fact she was merely slim, and nicely rounded, but to realise that you had to see her wearing next to nothing, which was fine by me.

A steward came to say that the captain would like a word with me, to sort out last-minute things before we reached home. With an effort I tore my eyes away from Della and went to the bridge.

It took only half an hour to deal with the details, then I hurried back to the pool to find that Della had gone.

'She went down to the cabin,' Jenny said. 'I think she wanted to make a phone call.'

I thought Jenny had probably got that wrong, because as far as I knew Della had nobody to phone. But when I approached the cabin I could hear her voice, obviously talking to someone.

'Darling, I didn't know—I wasn't expecting this yet—are you sure you're all right? Oh, that's wonderful—I can't wait to see you again. 'Bye, darling, bye.'

I heard her hang up.

I stood there a moment. For some reason I was reluctant to go in and see her. I wasn't sure why.

While I waited I heard a noise I didn't understand. If I'd been fanciful I might have thought she was crying. But that soft, gasping sound could have been anything—even my imagination.

Why should she cry? It had been a happy phone call. She'd said 'that's wonderful'. When I went in she would tell me what it was all about.

When I opened the door she was standing at the window, looking out to see. She turned and gave me a brilliant smile. And if it looked a bit forced, I decided that was my imagination too. I'd started seeing ghosts around every corner, and no other woman had ever made that happen to me.

'All right?' I said.

'Fine,' she said brightly. 'Never better.'

'Jenny told me you'd come down here. She said something about a phone call.'

'Yes, I needed to make one, but everything's all right now. Come on, let's go back to the pool. I need another swim.'

She sashayed past me and for a moment I was distracted by the sight of her smooth golden skin. I'd already admired it earlier that day, but each time was like seeing it for the first time.

So I forgot that she hadn't told me about the phone call and followed her tamely and happily back to the pool. Which, I realised later, was exactly what she'd meant me to do.

In the water she was like a mermaid, diving and twisting, always just ahead of me, teasing, tantalising, driving me off my head. I'd never wanted her as much as I did right then, and time was passing. Being a perfect gentleman had been fine while there was all the time in the world, but we would soon be in port.

In the late afternoon we docked at Southampton. Cars were waiting, goodbyes were said. Grace gave me her blessing in her own inimitable way.

'Whatever happens, you've brought it on yourself.'

I grinned. 'Thanks, Gracie.'

'And don't call me Gracie.'

Instead of eating on board I took Della to a tiny waterfront restaurant where the lights were low and the atmosphere intimate. Corny stuff, but it was an evening of sheer delight.

'I never did manage it, did I?' I asked her. 'I thought I could find out all about you, but you covered your tracks so well it's like you don't have any tracks.'

She didn't rise to it, and I suppose by that time I knew that she wouldn't. Her mysteries were too well concealed, but I could bide my time. So when she just smiled at me, I smiled back.

'Why does it matter?' she asked. 'I did my job well, didn't I?'

'Is that all it was? A job?'

'You hired me, at a very generous rate of pay.'

'I hired you when we were strangers,' I reminded her. 'But we're not strangers any more.'

'No,' she whispered, and I wondered if I only imagined that she sounded sad.

Suddenly I made my mind up. No more fooling. I knew what I wanted.

'Della, I don't ever want us to be strangers again. I want to marry you.'

From her startled look I knew she hadn't foreseen this, although I couldn't think why. Lord knows that I must have made myself obvious.

'What did you say?' she asked faintly.

'I want to marry you. I'm in love with you. Surely that can't come as a surprise?'

'It does in a way,' she said slowly. 'You haven't acted like a man in love.'

'You mean I haven't pounced on you like a starving teenager? I can't tell you how often I've wanted to. I've watched you walking about that boat, and I've watched the other men slavering over you, and I haven't known how I kept my hands off you.'

'Oh, you kept your hands off me pretty well,' she said, with a slight edge on her voice that made my heart soar.

'Were you expecting anything else?' I asked.

'Well,' she said slowly, 'in the circumstances—'

'What circumstances? I was paying your salary and therefore you were bought and paid for? Who do you think I am? Hugh Vanner?'

My darling glared at me. 'Is that why you've been acting like a Boy Scout?'

'Well—yes. And why are you snapping at me? You ought to be pleased that I showed you some respect. We made a business deal and I had you trapped on that boat. You were vulnerable. How could I—?'

She smiled suddenly. 'Why, Jack, you're a gentleman.'

'Yes, heaven help me! I must be. But you were hardly in a position to fight me off—'

'I could have jumped overboard.'

'No, it doesn't do to repeat a good trick. Besides, if you'd escaped me the same way you did Vanner I'd really have felt like a worm. And if you'd said yes, how would I have known why? You might have felt it was part of the bargain, and that you ought—'

My words ran out in a kerfuffle of embarrassment. There was something about the kindly way she was regarding me that was even more unnerving than her furious glare a moment before.

'I'm making a pig's breakfast of this, aren't I?' I said miserably.

That made her laugh, and she shook her head so that her earrings danced.

'Can you really see me making love to you because I felt obligated?' she asked.

'I'll be honest. There've been moments when I wouldn't have cared why, as long as I had you in my bed. But those times didn't last. I'd take a cold shower and know that it had to be because you wanted me. And I wasn't sure if you did.'

'Haven't you sensed it?' she asked, looking surprised.

'Sometimes. But the messages were always conflicting.'

We were in a dark corner of the restaurant, not facing each other, but at right angles on a continuous seat. Without saying a word she leaned across and laid her lips on mine for a long moment, while the world went into a spiral of dizzy dancing and my heart kept time.

'Is that message clear enough?' she asked.

I nodded. I couldn't trust myself to speak.

When I thought I could manage it I returned to what was, for me, the important thing.

'Now you know why I want to marry you. I'm not interested in a one-night stand, or a passing affair. I want lifetime commitment on both sides. Please, Della, will you be my wife?'

I'd been so sure she would say yes after that kiss, but she didn't answer for a moment. Then she said slowly, 'Don't ask me for an answer just now, please, Jack. I think you proposed on impulse, and you might regret it.'

'I won't change my mind.'

'But you know nothing about me.'

'Not for want of trying to find out. You told me that you weren't married already, and nothing else matters.'

'But I might have—other obligations.'

A memory from that afternoon flitted briefly through my mind, someone called 'darling' whom she was looking forward to seeing. But I was on a high and I banished the thought into the wilderness.

They say there are none so blind as those who will not see. And I guess I was determined not to see.

'Whatever your obligations,' I said, 'I'll help you with them.'

She shook her head and made the first helpless gesture I had ever seen from her.

'Jack, I can't say yes—not right now. You don't understand—'

'Then help me to understand. I'm in love with you, and I think you're in love with me. What else is there?'

'So many things,' she whispered. 'We've been living in a little isolated cocoon, but when you return to your real life things will look different. You won't need me quite so much.'

'Are you daring to suggest that I want to marry you to protect me from Grace?'

'No, I think you can manage that by yourself. After this she'll start to understand that your no is final. But that leaves you free.'

'Free to marry you. My darling, there's one aspect of Bully Jack that's true. They say when he wants something he's like a terrier—never lets go. I want you, and I'm not letting go. Why do you doubt me? I love you. You're my heart's desire, the only woman I'll ever want and love, for the rest of my life. If I could believe that you feel the same—'

She stopped me with a finger over my lips.

'Let's go,' she said softly.

We walked back to the boat, our arms wrapped around each other, feeling our bodies move in perfect rhythm. Most of the ship's crew and staff had been allowed to leave, and those that were left kept a discreet distance. We might have been the last two people on earth, wandering through an enchanted ghost ship.

Our packing was done, and the cases had already been placed in a cupboard outside the bedroom. But Della insisted on taking a last look and came up with a prize.

'Look at this,' she cried, waving the dowdy nightdress of that first evening. 'I pushed it under the bed so that nobody saw it. I suppose I could wear it tonight.'

'Tonight?' It came out as a yelp of anguish.

'Well, there's nobody to fool any more.'

'Except ourselves,' I answered. 'Is that what we've been doing? Fooling ourselves? Please don't say it is.'

'I suppose it depends what reality is,' she mused, 'and how badly you want to get away from it.'

'No,' I said, in a voice that surprised even me, 'no more of that.'

'What?'

'No more enigmas. Now it's time for the truth between us. I need to know how you feel about me, finally. It matters. If the answer's no, I'll go and spend tonight in one of the other cabins. We've got them all now.'

Her lips twitched. Even now she was teasing me. 'You're threatening to sleep in Selina's cabin?'

'It's sure as hell the only way she'd ever get me in there,' I growled.

She chuckled, and it shook me into fragments, 'Is that all that "truth" means to you, Jack?'

'Della, if you're talking about what I think you are, it's the only truth I can think of at this moment. Maybe that makes me a shallow character. I don't know, and right now I don't care. I've offered you my commitment, and now I want to make love to you so badly that it's driving me crazy.'

Then came the thing I'd been looking for, the little smile, starting at the corner of her lovely mouth and slowly spreading over it, as though all the world was hers to laugh at.

She was laughing at me, big, stupid clown that I was. And everything was wonderful.

She moved towards me, still holding that hideous nightdress. I suppose I must have seized it and tossed it away, but I don't remember doing so. But I seized her—I remember that—and pulled her hard against me and kissed her in a frenzy.

I may have been fiercer than I meant to be because I was past my limits of endurance by then. But she didn't seem to mind my rough hands. From the way she pressed against me I could almost believe she wanted me as much as I wanted her.

I loved how she pulled open the buttons of my shirt, not coquettishly, but in a way that was rather businesslike. She just wanted it off. No nonsense. She'd probably have had my trousers off the same way, but I beat her to it.

We'd been naked together before, but it had been an act for Grace's benefit. This time she was really mine. She was going to marry me. She hadn't actually said so, but who needed the words? I could feel her consent in the soft movements of her hands over my chest, and the even softer movements of her lips, teasing mine.

No other woman made love like this, as if it came from the heart. Every caress, every whisper was a gift.

She was sweet and melting, heart-stopping and glorious. I thought I knew her body. I'd seen it so often in a bikini, and had it pressed against me for a fleeting moment on that first morning. Now I discovered that I didn't know it at all.

How could anything feel as smooth as her skin, or as delicate? I was several inches taller, but she solved that problem by standing on my feet and then going on tiptoe, so that my hands could rove more easily over her, rejoicing in hills and valleys. I wanted her more with every moment that passed.

I heard her whispering incoherent words that might have contained my name. I think I spoke her name, or maybe I only spoke words of desire. I'm not sure, because by that time I was beside myself.

When we were together on the bed her face happened to lie in a shaft of moonlight, so that I could see her expression, and it startled me. There was a wildness that I'd never seen before, almost as though she were far away in another world, and not here with me at all.

There was wildness, too, in the way she made love, with nothing held back, inviting me into herself with whole-hearted passion, welcoming me to the heart of her.

We lay together a long time, and when we draw apart it was to return again almost at once. And when desire had abated the love was still there, as bright as ever—brighter, perhaps, now that it was all that was left. We slept in each other's arms.

I awoke after an hour, convinced I'd heard the noise of weeping. I listened, but there was only silence.

Beside me, Della lay facing in the other direction. I leaned over her.

'Are you all right?' I whispered.

She made a muffled sound, then resumed her deep, even breathing.

I settled down again, snuggling up with my arm around her.

When I next awoke it was in the half-light. I'd dreamed of her, and now my dream ran into my waking vision. I wanted her as much as ever.

'I'm incorrigible,' I said aloud. 'I ought to be ashamed of myself.'

Somehow I'd been certain that she would awake at the same moment, and I waited for the enchanting little chuckle I adored. It didn't come, and suddenly I was aware of some quality in the silence that made me nervous. I switched on the light.

The bed was empty.

There was nobody in the bathroom either.

I toyed with the idea that she might have gone up on deck: anything to avoid facing facts, I suppose. But I had to face them when I saw the letter that she'd left propped up on the dressing table. It was addressed simply *Jack*.

I stared at it for a long time before I opened it, because I didn't want to know what it said. Even though I already knew.

Forgive me for leaving you this way, but I'm afraid if we talked face to face I might lose my nerve.

It's been a wonderful time, so wonderful that it was unreal. Now it's time for reality again, and that's where we have to cease to exist for each other. I can't cross into your life, and you can't cross into mine.

I cannot marry you, my darling, but I will always treasure the fact that you asked me.

Perhaps I should have left without making love to you, and I tried to. I really did. But I couldn't make myself refuse. I think you know why. We met for a little time, and it was perfect. We'll always have that.

But it's all we can have. Let's not spoil it by asking for more.

I've taken the clothes you bought me, and Charlie. But I couldn't take the rest of the jewels. You'll find them locked in the second drawer down on the right.

I hope I gave you something. If I did, it's nothing to what you gave me. I won't spoil it by harming you, which is what I would do if I stayed in your life. I'll never forget you, but I can never see you again. I can't tell you why.

One last thing. Please, please don't try to find me. It would be no use, and I truly beg you not to try, because if you found me it would break my heart.

Dearest Jack, goodbye. Goodbye.

Della.

I never knew what winded in the gut meant until I read that letter. For a while I just didn't believe it. It hadn't happened because it couldn't have happened.

We'd found our dream and it would go on and on. Wasn't that how the story was supposed to end?

But dreams don't come true like that, and Della, being a woman, was more of a realist than me.

Maybe my mistake came from having too much money. For too long I'd snapped my fingers and what I wanted had been served up on a plate. I'd known straight off that I couldn't treat her like that—something about the way she kicked my shins, I think—but I'd become used to the luxury of always having her there.

Now it was time for the real world again, and I didn't like it.

The hints she'd dropped about her other life made me realise how well she'd kept her secrets. I'd angled and teased and fooled myself that I was learning something. But now she'd gone and I didn't know where to start looking—even if she hadn't begged me not to.

I checked the drawer, and of course the jewellery was all there, just as she'd said, because she was the most honest person alive.

I dressed and went out to find someone who was up. The sailor on watch was young and not very bright. He told me cheerfully that Miss Martin had left an hour ago.

'I called a taxi for her, and helped her with her bags.'

'Did she say why she was leaving so early?'

'She said there'd been a sudden change of plan and she had to leave urgently. She also said you didn't want to be disturbed. I hope you weren't, sir?'

'No, I definitely wasn't,' I said heavily.

He was like an eager puppy, expecting a pat on the head for devastating my life. I resisted the temptation to say he should have awoken me whatever she'd said. He wasn't my policeman.

I packed the jewels with a heavy heart. With any other woman I'd expect her to come back for the goodies, but not this one. She didn't want goodies.

I only wished I'd known what she did want. I might have found a way to give it to her.

CHAPTER EIGHT

Jack's Story

AT SOME point over the black months that followed I allowed myself to remember the thing
I'd been shutting out.

'Darling…I can't wait to see you again.'

I'd been in denial about the words I'd over-
heard, even though she'd vanished a few hours
later. Now I had to face it.

She'd left me for someone else. She'd de-
ceived me.

I didn't believe that.

'Darling…I can't wait to see you again.'

Then I went into denial again. Whatever the
truth, I couldn't bear to believe her anything
but honest.

It would have been easy to put an enquiry
agent on her tail, but that was the one thing I
couldn't do. She'd implored me not to, and if
I went storming after her all she would see
was that I disregarded her feelings when it
suited me.

She had said that if I found her it would break her heart. So I had nothing left but to obey her wishes without the solace of her presence.

I know my staff thought I was unusually tetchy. It wasn't like me, but I couldn't help it these days.

Do I have to say that I made money hand over fist? I couldn't breathe without making money. It was depressing.

Raymond Keller became head of Consolidated and, contrary to Grace's dire predictions, immediately made a deal with Bullen Inc, just as if I hadn't thumped him. I'd have liked to refuse, but it would have damaged too many people, so I set Stuart to do the negotiations.

Stuart is my right-hand man, and far more like 'Bully Jack' than I am. He was rather shocked that I'd taken time off for that cruise. He thought having fun was a waste of time. Only business mattered.

Having left him to do the deal, I then arranged to be away for the celebrations. Stuart represented me at those too—and did it very well, considering how festivities bored him.

The year moved on, the weather grew colder, and sometimes it was hard to remember that I'd ever cruised the Mediterranean in the sun.

Selina announced her engagement to Derek Lamming.

Grace said it was all my fault.

They married in December. I sent them an indecently generous wedding gift, which made Jenny giggle and say, 'There's no need to make your relief quite so obvious.'

Jenny always had a gift for hitting the nail on the head.

She looked at me anxiously. 'Are you all right, Jack?'

'Of course. Why?'

'You look older. You're not really all right, are you?'

I shrugged. I wasn't so good with the words these days.

'How's my future godson?' I asked, to change the subject.

She patted her stomach happily.

'Getting ready to make a grand debut. It was the yacht, you know. Those three days Charles and I vanished.'

Soon after that I slipped away. It was a subject I couldn't bear to talk about.

Over Christmas I invented a pile of work that had to be done, and managed to persuade Grace to spend the festive season with Harry.

Winter became spring, and I told myself that I ought to be well over Della by now. But I wasn't, and I began to be afraid that it would never end.

Grace lost patience with me and, being Grace, showed it in a way that felt like being kicked in the head.

I spent less time in our house now, but I was still there some days. One evening, as we sat over dinner, she leaned over and set something down before me.

It was Charlie.

'That is the brooch you bought her, isn't it?' she said in a smug tone.

I'd have liked to deny it, but there was the slight bend in the pin where I'd trodden on it. There was no doubt that this was the brooch I'd bought Della.

'I found it in a pawnshop,' Grace said triumphantly. 'She's sold it outright.'

I turned it over and over in my fingers, keeping my face stony so that Grace shouldn't see how much this hurt.

'Now will you see sense?' she asked. 'You had a lucky escape.'

I tried to keep my temper. It was harder these days.

'That's your view, Grace, but mine is different. I don't know why she did this, but I wish she'd come to me.'

'A cheap little floozie—'

She stopped because I met her eyes quickly. I recalled Charles telling me that I'd become scary these days. I'd dismissed it, but now the way Grace fell silent made me wonder.

'It's natural that you should be sentimental about her,' she said at last, a little more carefully. 'But she was very damaging to you.'

'You don't know that,' I growled.

'As a matter of fact, I do. I've found out who she is and, more important, what she is.'

'Are you going to tell me that you know where—?' I demanded in disbelief.

'Oh, yes, I know her whereabouts. That was the easy part.'

'And you didn't tell me?'

'Would you have thanked me for telling you that she's in prison?'

For a moment I was winded. Then I recovered and snapped, 'Nonsense.'

'It isn't nonsense. Pearl told me. She was visiting someone there and saw her.'

Pearl is Grace's maid and had seen Della on the boat. This story began to have a horrible likelihood about it, but I still said mechanically, 'I don't believe it.'

'Oh, I have no patience with you! Then believe this. After Pearl told me what she'd seen I hired a private enquiry agent.'

'I expressly forbade you to do that,' I said furiously. 'I told you she wouldn't like it.'

'Yes, and now we know why. You'd never have seen through her if I hadn't done something. I've found out things about your precious Della that explain exactly why she kept so quiet.'

She stopped there, waiting. In truth I was in agony, but hell would freeze over before I was going to ask her.

At last she repeated, 'Oh, yes, there are things she didn't want you to know, and I'm not surprised.'

'That was her choice,' I said curtly. 'When I see her, perhaps she'll choose to tell me.'

'She won't have much choice in prison, will she?'

My control broke.

'What the blazes is she doing there?'

'She's a crook.'

'Don't say that,' I told her angrily.

'Della Martin is on remand on a charge of stealing an extremely valuable diamond bracelet. She was caught red-handed. Apparently she comes from a notorious family of crooks. There's a whole gang of them—conmen, sneak thieves, pilferers. She was brought up dishonest. It's the only way she knows how to live. When I think that you invited her onto that boat to live with us— Anything might have happened.'

'I'll tell you what did happen,' I said furiously. 'I gave her a fortune in jewellery and she left it behind. No thief would do that.'

That took her aback for a moment, but then she shrugged her shoulders.

'Very clever. Of course you'd have sent the police after her if she'd taken everything.'

'No, it was hers to take,' I said coldly. 'And she knew it.'

I got up and prepared to go.

'I was only thinking of your best interests,' Grace protested.

'You have no idea what my best interests are,' I said, trying not to show just how angry I was. 'Grace, I don't want to quarrel with you. You're still my sister, and I love you, although right now I don't like you very much. I think it's best that I move out of here completely. Just tell me the name of the prison she's in.'

Grace pursed her lips.

'Wouldn't it be better if—?'

'*Tell me.*'

'Are you out of your mind?' she cried. 'Do you want people to know you associate with a jailbird? What will that do for your reputation?'

'Don't force me to ask Pearl,' I said quietly. She told me. She was very pale.

I promised myself I'd make it up and be nice to her later, but just now I couldn't bear the sight of her. Her pleasure in Della's misfortune revolted me.

Grace had one parting shot as I left the room. 'Just think about the share price,' she wailed.

There was only one answer to that, and I made it. 'To hell with the share price.'

It was a great exit line, and I'd like to say that I lived up to it. But I didn't. Not entirely.

I did the right things. I read the enquiry agent's report closely and noted the name of her lawyer. My phone call to him was a depressing experience.

'She's only my client because I was the lawyer on duty when she was arrested,' he told me feebly. 'In fact I can hardly be said to be representing her at all since she refuses to cooperate. She told the police her name and nothing else. That's all she told me, too. When we went before the magistrates she wouldn't talk to them—not even to say not guilty—'

'But she can't have stolen anything,' I interrupted him.

'Since she won't speak, I have no way of knowing,' he replied grimly.

He'd washed his hands of her and was merely going through the motions. I hated him. I told him to fix me a visit with her at the prison. He hummed and hah-ed. I talked money. He said to consider it done.

In the end I was told I could go the next day, and a permit arrived by messenger.

It was in the name of Smith. I'd arranged that in case she refused to see me.

That was when everything went pear-shaped.

I sat staring at that permit, wondering if I really meant to go. It was nothing to do with Grace's worries about my reputation. To hell with that! If people didn't trust me by now they could do the other thing.

No, it was something else.

I'd have treated her like a queen and she'd thrown it all back in my face, without even a proper goodbye.

And for what? To go back to a way of life where she couldn't even cope? So now she needed my help and I was supposed to come running. She could think again.

Dignity.

A man has his pride.

No, something else.

Sheer childish resentment?

That was it.

I had a heavy meeting next day, and no certainty of how long it would run. It was a big deal—good for me, good for the other side, on the right terms. Jimmy Haflin was a tough negotiator, but I knew I could get the better of him, eventually.

It was good-humoured, but it went slowly, and as the minutes ticked by I knew I couldn't make that visit. Given just a little more time I'd nail Jimmy down to everything I wanted, and that had to be my priority.

If I wasn't out of there by one-thirty I could forget it. And Jimmy dragged things out, almost as if he knew.

'I'm hungry,' he said at last. 'Why don't we finish this off over a decent meal?'

That would work in my favour. Jimmy was never at his best after the second glass. It was all going my way.

One-thirty.

'Sorry, Jimmy, no can do. I have to be out of here.'

'What? But we haven't settled anything.'

'Yes, we have. Five per cent is OK by me. We'll agree on that.'

'But you said five per cent was robbery.'

'So I've had a rethink. I can see you're not going to budge, so I give in. You sure are some tough negotiator.'

I think I was babbling by that time. Certainly my secretary was giving me a very strange look.

'Mary,' I said, rising and packing papers

away, 'please call the garage and tell them to have my car ready to go in two minutes.'

After that I got out fast, leaving her to deal with Jimmy's bewilderment and her own. If I hurried I could just make it in time.

The prison was in one of the most bleak and depressing parts of town, and I began to realise that it had been a mistake to bring the Rolls. I was attracting too much of the wrong sort of attention.

Then I forgot it. I was going to see Della again, and I was nervous.

I got more nervous when I went in. I'd never been inside a prison before, apart from a few unfortunate misunderstandings in my younger days, when I'd enjoyed myself a little too much. But that had been a few hours in a police cell. This was real. Worst of all, it was real for her.

When a severely uniformed warder said, 'This way, Mr Smith,' I was certain that she knew Smith wasn't my real name. Maybe everyone knew. Half the visitors to this place probably used that name, and they saw through all of us.

I'd had nightmare visions of talking through a glass screen, maybe even having to use a phone, like they do in films. But Della was on remand, and it was a relief to find a room with small tables and nothing between us.

I watched the door and saw when she entered. The shock was enough to make me rise out of my seat and start towards her in instinctive protest. How could they have done this to my Della?

She was in an old sweater and jeans, her hair cut even shorter than I remembered. Where once she'd looked gamine now she merely looked despairing. Her face, which had always been pale, now seemed bleached, and the black smudges of her eyes showed how long she had been without proper sleep.

I wanted to howl. Instead I forced a smile onto my face and took a step towards her.

The result was electrifying. She stopped dead and her face went, if possible, even whiter then before. Then she threw up her hands, as if warding off a monster.

It was the one thing I hadn't thought of. I'd guessed she might refuse to see me if she knew in advance, but I hadn't thought of her backing off when I was actually there.

'Della—' I said.

'No—no—I'm sorry, I can't. Go away, *please*.'

She turned and ran out. A warder went after

her, and another warder stood in front of me when I tried to follow.

'I'm sorry, you can't go through that door,' she said.

'But I've got to see her. Bring her back here.'

'We can't force her to see you.'

'But she's got to,' I said, trying to sound firm.

'No, she hasn't got to,' the warder said, also sounding firm, and doing it a lot more successfully.

'I won't leave without talking to her. You might tell her that.'

'I'll try, but she has the right to refuse.'

She spoke gently, like a mother to a rather stupid child. She looked about eighteen, and wasn't very large, but she was authority here. Suddenly I felt helpless and afraid—both feelings that I hated.

From the corridor outside I could hear desperate weeping. It tore me apart, and suddenly I didn't care about who gave the orders so long as I could get to see Della and make things right for her.

'Please,' I begged. 'Ask her to come back. Tell her I love her.'

She smiled. 'I'll tell her that.'

I recovered a little. 'And while you're at it tell her I won't leave without seeing her.'

I returned to the table and sat facing the door, my eyes fixed on it. It seemed like an eternity before she appeared, looking at me warily as she approached and sat down.

'You shouldn't have come,' she said.

I tried to make a joke of it. 'That's a fine thing to say after the trouble I took to— *Della!*'

I think my voice shook, and I must have sounded like a total wimp, so I pulled myself together.

'Never mind that,' I said briskly.

'But I do mind it. This was what I was trying to avoid—trouble for you. Oh, why couldn't you have left it there? I didn't want you to know all this.'

'Why not? Why couldn't you trust me?'

She gave a wan smile that tore my heart. I'd never seen anyone look so ill.

'Haven't you heard?' she asked. 'I'm a thief.'

'Don't talk damned nonsense!' I said violently.

'They caught me red-handed.'

'Oh, yes! With a diamond bracelet worth about a tenth of what you threw back at me. Frankly, my dear, as a jewel thief you have a lot to learn.'

I couldn't bear it. I tried to remind myself of the bad things about her—but I couldn't think of any. I just wanted to take her in my arms and promise to make everything all right.

'I meant it when I said you shouldn't have come,' she said tiredly. 'Why do you think I vanished? Because I knew I'd only damage you. You can't afford to be seen in a place like this. For pity's sake, go away.'

'Cut that!' I told her firmly. 'I want the truth and I'm not going until I get it.'

She looked surprised. I'd never spoken to her like that before. But by now I was desperate. She'd teased and tormented me long enough.

'Della, I know some of it, but I want you to tell me the rest.'

'What do you know?'

'About your family. Grace—'

She stopped me with a little gasp of laughter.

'Oh, well, say no more. I expect she did a thorough job. Detective agency?'

'I'm afraid so,' I admitted reluctantly. 'But what did you expect when she found you'd pawned Charlie?'

She couldn't look at me then. 'I'm sorry,' she mumbled. 'I didn't want to do it, but I needed the money.'

'Then why the devil didn't you take the rest

of the jewellery?' I snapped. 'You could have sold that and made some real money.'

'I couldn't take it,' she snapped back. 'It was—too much. I kept Charlie because—well, I told you why.'

'Sentimental reasons,' I said, speaking with heavy irony, because it was easier to cope that way. 'Until the day you sold it.'

'I had to sell it.'

'If you needed help why didn't you come to me?'

'Because I'd rather die.'

'Thanks,' I snarled. 'I'm not sure what I did to deserve that, but it tells me where I stand.'

'If it makes you go away it'll do its job very nicely.'

'But it won't make me go away, so get used to that.'

She glared at me, but didn't reply.

'Let's start again,' I said at last. 'Tell me about your family.'

'I don't suppose there's much you don't know after reading that report. We're a load of crooks.'

'*All* of you?'

She shrugged and made a face. 'It's what I grew up with. It wasn't called dishonesty, it was called ''making the best of your opportunities''. Stealing from the rich didn't count: they had plenty to spare.'

'And that's what your parents taught you?'

'I didn't know my parents. I told you they both died when I was two. Grandad raised me. He wasn't quite the same as the others. He was dodgy but he tried not to be, especially for my sake. He said he couldn't afford to go to jail because of having to look after me. He's a wonderful man and I love him to bits. Remember you told me about your Grandpa Nick, and I said my Grandad was the same? He really meant it about going straight for my sake. He didn't always stick to it, but he tried.'

'Last year he had a sort of ''final fling'' and ended up in prison. I was determined not to let that happen again, so while he was away I worked hard to earn as much money as possible and save it, so that when he came out we'd have enough.'

'You mean you'd have enough to support him?'

'And why not?' she flashed. 'He supported me all those years.'

'Was that what you were doing when we met?'

'Yes. He was due out very soon. The day before I left you I called home and found him there. He'd been released early so I had to get back.'

'I heard you. Do you mean that he was ''darling''?'

'Yes.'

'I wish you'd told me what was happening.'

'You were the very last person I wanted to know. Have you any idea what it does to me to see you here, know what you're thinking?'

'You can't begin to imagine what I'm thinking,' I said harshly. 'Tell me what happened when you got home.'

'We were fine for a while, but then the money ran out. I sold my new clothes, and we lived well on them for a while. The trouble was that I couldn't get a job. I couldn't leave him alone at home because he got depressed, and then—' She gave a tired shrug.

'I thought he'd get better, but he didn't, and the money got lower. That's when I pawned Charlie. I thought I'd be able to redeem him, but things got worse so I had to sell him outright.' She looked away from me. 'I hated doing that.'

I think I hit rock-bottom at that moment. I'd known this woman feisty, unafraid, cheeking everyone—especially me. Now she couldn't look me in the eye, and that hurt like hell.

'Anyway, Grandad tried to do his bit. He got

a job as a waiter in a hotel. He started on lunches, and did so well that they promoted him to evenings. That was the trouble.'

'How do you mean?'

'It's in the evenings that people wear diamonds. There was this woman in a diamond bracelet, and the clasp must have come undone. Anyway, Grandad says he found it on the floor when they were clearing up later, and just couldn't resist. As soon as he told me I knew I had to return it—fast. So that's what I did, but it all went wrong.'

'You don't mean you took it back yourself?' I demanded, aghast. 'Just walked in there and—?'

'Yes,' she said, looking at me truculently.

'But that's not the way,' I said. 'You should have sent it by mail.'

'Suppose it hadn't got there?'

'You send it Special Delivery and you protect yourself from discovery by going to a post office where you aren't known and giving a false address.'

I stopped because she was staring at me.

'What is it?'

'You sound like one of my family. They know all the tricks too. My Uncle Alec would have said the same.'

'It's a pity you didn't consult him, then.'

'I did. And he told me not to worry, that he'd
return it for me. As though I was born yesterday! I said he wasn't getting his thieving paws
on it, and we had a row and I stormed out.

I groaned. 'Your family are a big help, aren't
they?'

'You leave my family alone,' she flashed.
'They are what they are. It's nothing to do with
you.'

'I won't even try to answer that. Just tell me
what happened next. You tried to return the
bracelet, right?'

'Yes, only I had to be clever and waltz in
there when the place was crawling with police.
And—how's this for luck?—one of the police-
men knew the family and recognised me. So
then he makes me turn out my pockets, and
there's the bracelet.'

'Why didn't you just say all this?' I demanded, nearly tearing my hair.

'Because I can't split on Grandad.'

'Great. You're loyal to him, but where's his
loyalty to you? Why doesn't he come forward
with the truth?'

'Because I've told him not to. Don't you
see? It wouldn't help. They caught me with the
stuff on me. If he confesses it wouldn't help
me. They'd just have both of us. And he can't
go back to prison. He'd die.'

'But it's all right for you to get locked up, is it?'

'No, but I can't help it,' she said. 'There's nothing to be done. Why don't you just go?'

'Perhaps I should,' I snapped back. 'At least while you're here I know where you are and what you're up to.'

'Fine! Then we're both happy.'

'Don't talk nonsense. From now on you've got to be sensible.'

'Meaning what?'

'Meaning that you do it my way. Give me your home address—I mean, please.'

'You're not to make trouble for Grandad.'

'I'm trying to save him as well as you. He needs you on the outside, looking after him. Otherwise he'll do something else stupid.'

She nodded wretchedly and I realised that this thought had tormented her. She was trapped, unable to defend herself properly for fear of hurting the old man she loved, but knowing that whatever she did would probably be bad for him. And I hadn't been there to help her. The thought made me feel savage.

'Write your address there,' I said, pushing paper and pen towards her. 'And when I send a lawyer here don't refuse to see him.'

'I already have a lawyer.'

'You haven't. I just fired him.'

'Oh, really? Bully Jack is showing his teeth now, is he?'

'You'd better believe it. From now on Bully Jack is going to bully to some purpose. Starting with getting you out on bail.'

'I don't want bail.'

'You'll do as you're damned well told.'

That made her stare. She wrote the address down and pushed the paper towards me.

'The lawyer will call soon,' I said, pocketing it. 'Do everything he tells you, and sign a paper authorising him to tell me anything I want to know.'

'He'll tell you anyway.'

'True, but let's keep things legal.'

I regretted the words as soon as they were out.

'You had to put it like that, didn't you?' Della asked bitterly. *'Keep things legal.* You simply had to say it.'

'It was a slip.' I backtracked hastily. 'Just a meaningless phrase.'

'It was you stomping all over me with your size nines, *Bully Jack.*'

'Oh, great! And that was something *you* had to say, wasn't it? OK, you've had your revenge. I'm going. I'll be in touch.'

Why did I bother? Why did I take such trouble for a sulky, ungrateful, sharp-tongued female? Asking these questions of myself, I stormed out of the prison and around the corner.

And there was my Rolls, with all the tyres removed.

CHAPTER NINE

Della's Story

Look, I've got a great family, OK? They're not quite like anyone else's family, but they're great. Especially Grandad.

My mother was his daughter, and the person Grandad loved best in all the world after his wife had died. When she got married everyone in the family thought Grandad would hate sharing her, but he and my father took to each other from the first.

They shared the same vice—gambling. Nothing serious. Just the odd visit to the bookies and a bit too much wagered on how fast a horse or dog could run. Kindred spirits.

They moved in with him, everyone lived happily until I was born, and then they were even happier. It lasted for three years. Until Mum and Dad died together in a car crash. After that, as I'd told Jack, Grandad raised me.

It took a while for me to understand that I came from a family of crooks. Or, as Uncle

Alec used to say, we lived on the edge. He meant the edge of the law, the edge of a jail sentence.

Alec's speciality was insurance fraud, or what he called 'victimless crime'.

'Who loses?' he'd cry. 'So maybe they put a penny on the premiums, but nobody notices that.'

Grandad would frown in a puzzled way, but he wasn't great at arguing things through. And Alec could always silence him with a wink and a compliment about our new kitchen. Recently an insurance firm had replaced everything after a fire under a chip pan had covered the old one with soot. It now looked really lovely.

I'd been away staying with friends at the time, so I hadn't seen the fire, but I knew Grandad didn't like it mentioned.

Someone who could really argue the toss was Uncle Harry. He was a lawyer, and the one really respectable member of the family. He lived a good, decent life, paid his taxes without a murmur and maintained honest values.

The problem was his wife, who seemed to have a poor sense of direction and kept walking into doors. Alec loathed Harry. He kept making barbed remarks like, 'Nobody's ever seen my wife with a black eye.'

Which was true. Him, maybe. Her, never.

I was fond of Alec, and when he said that Harry was a poor advertisement for honesty I had to agree.

Their father was Grandad's brother, Tommy, who used to refer to himself sentimentally as 'one of the old-style villains', trying to sound like the Godfather. Grandad said he was just a small time con artist who made a mess of everything he touched, but he had status because he'd been around so long and had done more time than anyone else. This didn't seem to me a great recommendation, but my family sees things in their own way.

Tommy had six offspring, five of whom had gone into the business, and *their* offspring had followed. So I guess that made us a dynasty.

They lived by low-level crime, usually starting with shoplifting when they were under ten. Aunt Hetta: now there was an expert! She'd go into a big store with her three daughters, who'd collect things and deliver them to her. The cameras would pick up the kids, but they were always clean by the time they left the store. Aunt Hetta would sail out, loaded to the teeth, with nobody taking any notice of her.

She took me on one of these raids when I was eight, and I was really good at it. But then Grandad found out and hit the roof. I heard part of the row he had with Hetta, although I didn't understand much. He said if he caught her leading me astray again he'd make her sorry she was born. She said he was depriving me of the family heritage.

'How's the poor girl ever going to earn a decent living if she doesn't learn now?' she wailed.

Grandad had been raised amongst all this, but he always claimed that he swore to go straight when I was growing up because he didn't want to get sent to jail and have me put in care.

Like everything he said there was a pinch of truth in there, buried deep under a load of tinsel.

We lived reasonably well, because Grandad would occasionally have a big win on 'the gee-gees'. But the wins were too big and too regular to be pure chance.

Later I realised that he had friends who knew what was going to win and tipped him off. I met one of them once, and he winked and said. 'I like to pay my debts.'

But he wouldn't say what Grandad had done to be repaid. Or when. Grandad wouldn't say either.

He supplemented his wins with a few cash-in-hand jobs at a builder's yard, plus, of course, all the state benefits he could apply for. Harry, being a lawyer, was a big help with getting the forms and telling him what to say on them. Alec said it was the only time in his life Harry ever did anything useful.

This was Grandad's notion of 'going straight'. I learned early on that he had his own version of everything. No story was ever quite as he said, but always embellished to make it more entertaining. To a child this seemed wonderful. So what if he was a bit dodgy? All right, more than a bit. How easy do you think it is for a man who was raised to be a crook to suddenly go straight?

He gave me a happy, magical childhood, and the security of knowing that he loved me without limit and I loved him without limit. And there was no more to be said.

Sometimes he'd get sentimental about the old days and want a 'final fling'. Since he was useless at it he always got caught and went away for a few months.

When this happened I'd live with my cousins, who'd gone into white-collar crime and were big-time now. I'd live in their flash houses, receive expensive presents and go on their luxurious holidays.

That was how I discovered high living, but, given that Grandad had raised me to be honest, it might have been better not to know about it.

I met a lot of the wrong people. Charmers, all of them, but you couldn't have a sustained relationship with someone who might vanish into jail at any time.

Then I set my heart on being an actress. I got almost no work, but Grandad assured me we were in the money and he could keep me going.

Of course that was one of his daydreams, and I ought to have known it. But I suppose I blinded myself to what I didn't want to know until I got a call from a police station. Grandad had returned to his old ways. It was a disaster. If he'd ever had any skills, which I seriously doubt, he'd forgotten them. He ended up behind bars and I did some thinking.

This was my fault. How was he supposed to stay on the straight and narrow when I was being a drain on him? He'd always looked after me, and now it was time for me to look after him.

I abandoned the theatre, which didn't seem to notice my departure any more than it had noticed my arrival, and I got jobs demonstrating in stores. I lived as frugally as possible, saving for when Grandad came home.

I saw him on every visiting day, and it broke my heart to see him in that place. He was too old for prison, and I had to keep his spirits up by talking about the times we'd have together when he was released.

On my last visit I'd told him about being a waitress on *The Silverado*.

'It's just for a few weeks,' I assured him. 'I'll come and see you as soon as I'm back in England. You'll be out soon after that, and we'll never let this happen again. Will we?'

'Never,' he said, holding up his hand. 'That's a promise.'

The trouble was, it had always been a promise. He was easy-going, and people could talk him into things.

So from now on I was going to be in total control of everything—my life, his life, the lot. No more nasty surprises.

And what did I have to go and do? Fall in love with a man I could never have. Brilliant!

Right from the start I knew Jack and I had no future.

It didn't matter that I'd never been a crook. Practically everyone else I knew *was*. Mud sticks. Jack might be a millionaire, but he couldn't afford me.

So our time together had to be something apart. I would enjoy, leave it, and remember it without bitterness.

I didn't know how long we'd have. Jack had wanted us to stay together for a while after we left the boat. I thought we might even have a month.

But then I called home and found that Grandad had been released early. So I had to return at once. I allowed myself that one last evening with Jack. I thought I could handle it, but he took my breath away by asking me to marry him. The one thing I'd never thought of.

For a few glorious moments I let myself dream. I've never wanted anything so much in my life, and I never will again.

But I couldn't say yes, for his sake. He made it hard for me by talking about love in a voice that seemed to wrap itself around my heart. If only, I thought, he would stop talking like that. If only he would never stop.

I made him give me a little time, just to put off actually saying no, which was going to break my heart.

Perhaps I shouldn't have made love with him, but I knew that if I didn't spend that night in his arms I'd regret it all my days.

I remember returning to our cabin after an evening at a little restaurant on the shore. There was some foolery with the dreary nightdress which I found pushed away under the bed, and he took it from me and tossed it away.

After that there was no going back. He grabbed me in a sort of frenzy. I suppose he was rough, but I didn't mind because I knew it was only frustration, and I was feeling it too. If he'd gone on being restrained I'd probably have thumped him.

I heard some material tear and thought it must be my dress. Actually it was his silk shirt, as I discovered when I stepped over it later.

But if he didn't rip my dress it was only because he didn't need to. He was an expert in removing delicate things without damage, but I was pulling my own clothes off at the same time as his.

I suppose we were naked at about the same moment, and that was like a confirmation that this was really going to happen at last. So then there was no need to rush to bed. There was time to stand there and feel our bodies against each other.

It was so good. I knew his body well from having spent so much time gazing at it. I knew the heaviness in his shoulders, the hint of power kept in reserve, seldom needing to be used. I knew the way his torso narrowed down to lean hips and long, muscular thighs. I could still feel him lying against me, as he'd done the first morning, his desire unmistakeable. I'd wanted him then and I wanted him now.

I brushed my lips across his chest, listening to his heartbeat, hearing it grow a little more urgent as I moved my hands over him. It was the same with me. As his fingers tips roved all over me, exploring, inciting, my pulse grew faster.

He was murmuring soft words. 'All my life—all my life—'

Did he mean that he'd waited for me all his life? Or that we would have a lifetime together? I couldn't afford to wonder. Too much grief lay that way. Tonight I was going to be his in every way I could. In my heart I was already his for ever, and I tried to show him in ways he'd remember later.

I said he was always in control, but he was losing it then, and that was wonderful. He'd asked me to be his wife, and this was as good as our wedding night, even though the wedding would never take place.

We walked slowly to the bed, not hurrying because the world and time were ours. He sat on the edge and drew me towards him, between his legs, so that he could rest his head against my breasts. I wrapped my arms about him, feeling strangely protective of this strong man.

I felt the tears come as I realised that he trusted me enough to be vulnerable to me. I knew I mustn't think of that. Not when I was about to betray his trust and desert him.

He kissed my breasts so gently, so lovingly,

that all sense of strain fell away from me. I was nothing now but this man's lover, with no purpose in life but to receive his love and give it back a thousandfold.

So I arched into him, clasping my hands behind his head and inciting him to love me with his tongue, his lips. And he did, again and again. I took deep breaths, bracing myself for the shattering, beautiful sensations that went through me.

But before long that wasn't enough. I wanted him to feel the same. So I drew him down on the bed, made love to him with all my heart, and had the happiness of feeling his response.

'Do you know how much I want you?' he whispered.

'Not until you show me,' I whispered back.

So he did, easing over me and accepting the welcome I offered him. We became one with mutual joy. I could see my own feelings mirrored in his eyes and I smiled, knowing that hc was as much mine in that moment as I was his.

And we were still each other's when he left me, because we lay for a long time holding on, making the moment last. Maybe I only imagined it, but I like to think we fell asleep in the same moment.

I awoke after an hour. It wasn't yet dawn, so I still had a little longer before life ended.

Jack was sleeping on his front, his face turned towards me, his lips moving slightly as he breathed.

I kissed him. He didn't stir, and I kissed him again, then again, saying goodbye. I tried not to cry, but I was never going to see him again and I couldn't stop. A tear fell on his face. I dried it quickly and turned over to muffle the rest in the pillow.

Behind me I heard him stir and move closer to me, saying softly, 'Are you all right?'

I muttered and buried my face deeper in the pillow. I didn't want him to know I was crying.

I felt him settle down and go to sleep against me, his arm over me. Oh, Jack, Jack!

I took the coward's way, slipping out in the dawn without waking Jack. He'd moved by then, and I was able to ease my way out of the bed without disturbing him.

After the loving we'd had it was cruel to leave him like that. It had probably been cruel to make love to him at all, but I wasn't strong enough to do anything else. After Jack, life was going to be a bleak vista of greys, and I would need that night to help me through it.

Luckily he's a heavy sleeper, and I was able to write my letter, dress and slip out without him knowing. I took a taxi to the railway station and a train to London, heading for Uncle Alec's house and reaching it just before lunch.

Grandad was there, actually looking out of the window, and the sight of his face when he saw me made me feel for a moment that all the pain was worth it. I wasn't always going to believe that, but I did at that moment. When the front door was opened he flung his arms around me, and I could actually feel him sobbing with relief.

I did a bit of crying too. It was so good to have him back, and now he was all I had to love.

Let me try to show him to you. Imagine Father Christmas—big white beard, twinkling eyes, the lot. At first sight he comes across as naïve and gullible, which part of him is. But there's more to those eyes than a twinkle. He knows, as the saying goes, how many beans make five. He also knows how to pretend they're six.

That's my grandad. Great-hearted, generous, lovable, shrewd, dodgy, wildly unreliable and slightly potty.

'Where've you been, girl?' he asked, wiping his eyes. 'I've missed you.'

'I've missed you too,' I said huskily. 'I told you I was working on a ship. I left it at

Southampton this morning and came straight
here.'

'Yeah, I remember you telling me now. Do
well out of it, did you?'

I didn't bother him with the details of how
I'd changed ships. He didn't need to know.

'Yes, I did pretty well,' I said cheerfully.

By this time the rest of the family were col-
lecting around us. Most of them had come there
today, so that we could have a party to celebrate. Alec, Hetta, more uncles and several of
my cousins. Not all, of course, because two
were unavoidably detained.

The mood was very jolly. They noticed the
suitcases Jack had bought me, and their obvious value caused some comment. When I
opened one to take out a dress for the party
there were cheers as they viewed the contents.

'Here, girl, you found yourself a millionaire
or what?'

'Or what!' I said, trying to laugh. 'Definitely
what!'

Maria, Hetta's eldest daughter, held up one
of the other dresses and twirled with it.

'Don't suppose your ''what'' has any brothers?' she asked.

'No, he's unique,' I said.

All three of Hetta's daughters were into full-
time shoplifting now, and doing very well at it.

Lisa had tried something more sophisticated—computer hacking and stealing credit card numbers on-line. But she didn't have a gift for it and made such a mess of things that she had to dump a valuable laptop in a lake to get rid of the evidence. At least, she thought it was valuable. She hadn't been able to ask the price when she obtained it, but she'd seen one like it in a catalogue.

So she rejoined her sisters in the shops, and was soon back in business. The family were dead proud of them all. Hetta was especially proud of Lisa, who'd tried to broaden her horizons and 'dream her dreams'.

'She may have made a mess of it, but you've got to hand it to her for trying,' she said.

'Are you all right, luv?' Grandad asked me halfway through the evening.

'Yes, I'm fine.'

'Only, you're just staring into space.'

'I guess it all feels a little weird to hear them talking that way, as though it's the same as any other career. At any minute I expect to hear that they're going to have a convention and an awards scheme.'

'Well, I wouldn't win any awards for that last job,' he said with a sigh.

'No, and there aren't going to be any more,' I told him firmly. 'You've retired.'

It was a good party. Grandad and I stayed
the night, but we were both looking forward to
leaving next day and getting back to our own
home. It was a tiny rented apartment in South
London. Nothing grand, but it was cosy, and
even now I loved it. We'd been happy there.

The first day at home wasn't too bad because
there was so much to do. Cleaning, buying
food, making lots of tea and chatting while we
drank it. After the jollity of the night before
Grandad was a bit quiet, and once he just
stopped what he was doing and flung his arm
around me. I comforted him as I would have
done a child, because that was what he was
now. He was my child and I was going to protect him.

But when it was time to go to bed and
found myself alone there were no more de
fences against what was happening inside me
I loved Jack, and I'd walked away from him
It was for ever. No going back.

If I should weaken I had only to remember
the party yesterday—crooks, con merchants
jailbirds, all milling around swapping jokes a
if it was the most natural thing in the world
Even to mention Jack's name among them
could damage him, and I wouldn't do it.

Suddenly I felt colder than at any time in m

ife. I got up and turned on the heating. But I
vas still cold.

After that first salary cheque, Jack had given
ne another one, so for a while we had enough
o manage on. Just in case he was trying to
race me I opened a bank account in another
part of London and deposited the cheques
here. I half wondered if he would stop them,
ut that would have been spiteful, and not like
ack.

Sure enough, they cleared easily, and I drew
ut the money in cash to put it in my normal
ccount. Things were fine for a bit. I couldn't
et a decent job, because leaving Grandad
lone for long was too chancy, but I did some
art-time work. It didn't pay well. As the
noney ran out I began to sell my new clothes.

In the end the only thing I had left to sell
vas Charlie. I put it off as long as possible, but
here was no choice.

He was my last link with Jack, but I didn't
ry. I was beyond that. And besides, I had to
eep up a brave face for Grandad.

I thought I'd fooled him, but of course I
adn't. One day he went out alone, came home,
nd told me he'd got a job as a waiter.

'But you know nothing about being a
aiter,' I said, stunned.

'Yes, I do. My cellmate used to be head

waiter at—' He named a top London hotel. 'He
served royalty. He told me all about it.'

He did well at first. He was a good mimic
and picked up enough to get by. I thought per
haps our troubles were almost over.

But they were just beginning.

CHAPTER TEN

ella's Story

F COURSE I did everything wrong, and when
landed in jail I knew that only a miracle
ould rescue me.

How strange that the miracle should be
race, making one last attempt to turn Jack
ainst me and giving him the key to finding
e.

When I heard that 'Mr Smith' had come vis-
ng I thought it was one of my cousins, being
utious. And then I walked in and saw Jack.

I made a mess of it again. I should have been
erjoyed, thrown my arms around his neck,
ied, *Jack, darling, at last!*

Instead, I was filled with the most terrible
ar and misery. Perhaps I'd forgotten how to
el anything else. Anyway, I fled, and they had
stop him coming after me.

From the corridor outside I could hear him
gging them to bring me back. I leaned

against the wall, shaking, feeling my hea
pound. Even my teeth were chattering.

A warder came back and told me briskly th
I was mad.

'If I had a feller who looked like that yo
wouldn't catch me running away,' she sai
'Go on with you.'

So I went and sat down and, charming to th
end, said, 'You shouldn't have come.'

Fear and misery had given way to rage. Aft
I'd tried so hard to protect him he'd swept a
my efforts aside and walked into the lions' de
Had he *no* sense?

I think I said something like that—somethin
bad-tempered, anyway. He ought to hav
walked out, but he didn't. I remembered the
how stubborn he was when he'd decided c
something.

He looked different—thinner, older—ar
he'd lost that look of always having a smi
about to burst out. He smiled sometimes, but
was forced, and faded quickly. Then his mar
ner became curt and no-nonsense. He eve
snapped at me. I snapped back, and we we
soon squabbling.

I told him about my life in the months sin
we'd parted, but all the time I was wonderir
about his life, whether I was responsible for h

withered look, as though something were gnawing him from inside.

If I could have done as I wanted I'd have put my arms about him, promised never to go away again. But I couldn't. A block of ice seemed to be pressing on my chest, trapping the feelings inside. So I went on being grumpy and he went on giving his orders.

He'd fired my lawyer, he was hiring another, he wanted my address. I had to be sensible, leave it to him, just keep quiet and don't argue. Bully Jack was there with a vengeance.

I did what he wanted, then we rowed some more, and he left.

I didn't know what to think. At the back of my mind I knew things had taken a turn for the better, but I couldn't feel it. I didn't know this new version of Jack, or how to react to him.

My new lawyer was called Thomas Wendell. He came to see me that same afternoon, and the very next day I was back in court, pleading not guilty.

'But how can I?' I demanded. 'After they caught me red-handed.'

'Miss Martin, my instructions are that you were *not* caught red-handed, but merely the victim of a misunderstanding which will soon be sorted out.'

'Your instructions? From Mr Bullen, I suppose? What else did he say?'

'To get you out of here at all costs. Now, please speak as little as possible, and leave everything to me.'

Inside the court he put in my plea and asked for bail, but the magistrate was reluctant. He spoke of my lack of co-operation and suggested that I was liable to abscond.

In the end bail was set at thirty thousand pounds. An outrageous figure. Without batting an eyelid Mr Wendell agreed.

That told me all I needed to know. But it might have been worse. At least Jack hadn't actually turned up in court.

'What do I do now?' I asked as we left.

'You see that car over there, with the blacked-out windows? Just get in the back. Goodbye.'

'Hey, wait a—'

But he was already walking away, leaving me no choice but to go to the car.

Jack was there in the back, his face harsh with tension. He drew me inside, tapped the dividing screen, and an unseen chauffeur started up.

As we moved off Jack threw himself back into the far corner and just sat looking at me. The light was poor, and I couldn't see his face well, but I think it bore the saddest look I'd ever seen.

'Are you all right?' he asked.

'I'm better now. I'll be all right when I've seen Grandad.'

'I'm taking you to him. One moment.' His mobile phone had rung and he answered it curtly. 'Yes? I know, but I can't help it—you'll just have to handle the meeting yourself. You can do it, Peter. I trust you.'

When he'd finished I took a deep breath and started on the speech I knew I had to make.

'I'm sorry about the way I spoke to you when you came to see me. I'm really grateful for—'

'Shut up!'

His voice seemed to reach me across a vast distance.

'Don't thank me. Whatever you do, *don't thank me.*'

'I don't understand.'

'I can believe that,' he said, almost savagely.

Silence. A cold, bitter silence, between strangers.

'If I can't say sorry, what can I say?'

'Nothing. What is there to say?'

He sounded oddly defeated, and his shoulders sagged. I hated seeing him like that. He was my Jack, king of the world, who could sort out anything. Worst of all was the feeling that the person who'd brought him to this was me.

'This isn't the way home,' I said suddenly, startled.

'You don't live there any more. I'm taking you to my place.'

'But Grandad—'

'He's already there. I went to see him at the address you gave me as soon as I left the prison yesterday.'

I made an amazed gesture, which he understood.

'He was a little surprised, since you'd never mentioned me to him,' he said. 'But I told him what was happening, and we packed up and went.'

'How is he?'

'I found him fairly depressed. That's why I took him with me at once. I thought the less time he spent alone brooding the better.

'You mean he stayed at your place last night?'

'That's right.'

'Jack, what did you tell him?'

'Just that you worked on my boat. For all he knows you were a waitress. But we didn't talk much. We just got drunk.'

This was becoming more surreal every moment. I tried to imagine their meeting at our shabby little home, and in the end I gave up.

Nor could I picture Jack getting drunk. Grandad, yes.

The phone rang again. He answered impatiently, said, 'I'll be there in an hour,' and hung up.

We were in the heart of Mayfair now, gliding through residential streets that were quiet and unobtrusively wealthy. We stopped in front of an apartment block and I waited for him to get out. But he seemed frozen, staring at the floor as though lost in an unhappy dream.

'Why did you do it?' he said at last.

'I told you why in my letter. I had to go, and now surely you must know why?'

'There could have been a way around it if only you'd trusted me. Now—' He gave a dispirited shrug.

I knew what he was saying. It was too late—now. He was helping me for old times' sake, but he didn't want me to think it had anything to do with love.

I hastened to assure him that I had no such illusions.

'There was no way around it, Jack. I told you then. You can't be part of my life and I can't be part of yours. It was nice of you to come to my rescue, but the end still has to be the same.

Of course if I go to jail there won't be any prob—'

'That's enough!' he said violently, seizing my shoulders. 'Don't ever talk like that. Do you hear me? I forbid it.'

He shuddered, and I felt it go through his hands to my own flesh.

'I won't let it happen,' he said. 'Do you understand that?'

I reached up and took one of his hands, holding it between mine.

'Perhaps even Bully Jack can't manage this,' I said.

'If he can't, he isn't good for much. You're not going back to that place. You have my solemn word. Do you believe me?'

'Yes,' I said, almost hypnotised.

His face was blazing with fervour, and for a moment I could imagine him capable of anything. He could save me and Grandad. He could overturn the whole world.

'Della, if you believe in me—'

His voice was shaking. He would have said more but his phone rang again. It broke the spell, forcing him to seize it and answer with an edge on his voice.

'I'll deal with it as soon as I get in this afternoon.'

He opened the car door quickly, before the

phone could ring again, and we entered the building. His flat was on the third floor, and we went up in the lift, neither speaking nor looking at each other. After that brief, intense moment in the car we were both awkward.

As soon as I went in and saw Grandad I forgot everything else. He came flying to meet me, as he'd done on the day I came home, and we hugged each other silently. Jack didn't look at us, but went into another room to make a phone call. When he came out he spoke briefly.

'I have to leave now. Della, have something to eat and make yourself at home. Your grandfather will show you where everything is. I'll see you later.'

He was gone. Grandad and I hugged again. We'd seen each other only last week, when he'd visited me, but it was as though we'd been apart for months.

At last he wiped his eyes and sniffed.

'Last time it was me welcoming you home from jail,' I said, trying to lighten the atmosphere.

He straightened up. 'I'll make you a cup of tea, luv.'

'Yes, please. Prison tea is horrible.'

'You're telling me. You should try what they serve in—'

We slid easily into a discussion of prison tea

that we had known, and that got us over the next few minutes. He bustled about in Jack's kitchen, already at home.

'Baked beans on toast,' he said, knowing that was my favourite. 'I bought the beans specially for you this morning.'

While he cooked I looked around. Jack had made this place sound small, but maybe his idea of small wasn't everyone else's. It was light and spacious, with two bedrooms, a large bathroom, an office and one big living room.

'That's your room,' Grandad said, pointing.

It had a double bed and was furnished with discreet luxury in various shades of brown and fawn.

'Where are you sleeping?' I asked him.

I followed his finger and opened the door of the other bedroom, where there were two single beds.

'Grandad—?'

'Him and me have to share, luv. There's nowhere else. I don't mind.'

'*You* don't—?'

'As long as he doesn't snore.'

'He doesn't snore,' I said defensively.

Grandad nodded in a satisfied way. 'I thought you'd know about that.'

'I'll throw a baked bean at you in a minute.'

He cackled. 'Come and eat.'

While I was eating he said, 'You should've told me about him.'

'There was nothing really to tell.'

'You've got a millionaire nutty about you and there's nothing to tell?'

'He's not nutty about me. This is a gesture to a friend.'

'Pull the other one. He's turning his life upside down to look after you. Even I can see that.'

I said nothing, but my mind went back to the phone constantly ringing in the back of the car. How many meetings had he put off for my sake? What else was there?

'Did he give you all that stuff you brought home?' Grandad asked.

I nodded.

'Why didn't you ask him to help you?'

'Because I don't—' I started to say that I didn't want Jack's help, but the words faded.

'Yes, you do,' Grandad said. 'Because you're as nutty as he is.'

There was no arguing with him in this mood. When Grandad gets hold of an idea he's like a terrier with a bone.

I had a long, luxurious soak, feeling the prison wash away from me. Then I went to bed, slept for an hour, and awoke feeling more or less human again.

There was a suitcase in my room, filled with the packing that Grandad had done for me. I'd kept a few of the clothes Jack had bought me because they were good quality and useful, but I refused to put any of them on now. Instead I chose old jeans and a sweater. I think, in my daft way, I was trying to send him a message.

If I was, it fell flat. He came in about eight o'clock, nodded briefly to us, and vanished into the study. From there I could hear him constantly on the phone. When he emerged, about an hour later, Grandad said, 'Something to eat? Beans on toast?'

'That sounds good.'

He began knocking up the dish, assuring me that Jack loved it because he'd had it last night. My mind boggled at the thought of Jack eating Grandad's cuisine.

I managed to take him aside and say quietly, 'I'm sorry you have to share a room with him. I never thought of anything like that.'

'I don't mind. I just want you to be easy in your mind about him. Don't worry. He's going to be all right. And so are you.'

'Jack, I want to ask you something. Is that your room I'm sleeping in?'

'Of course. There was no other way of arranging it. Are you comfortable?'

'Yes, it's lovely in there. The bed's so soft. But—'

'Right, that's sorted that out. Is that food ready yet?'

Over the meal I could see that somehow they had become the best of friends. I guess there's something about getting pie-eyed together that forms a bond between men. Grandad launched into the story of his life, with embellishments.

'You'll never believe the fight I had to put up to keep her,' he said, glancing at me. 'One bloke looking after a baby on his own! Social Services weren't having that. They said they were going to take her and find her a foster home. I said, "Over my dead body". But they wouldn't give up. Came knocking at midnight, demanding that I hand my little girl over. I told them they'd have to take her by force.'

Glancing up, I caught Jack's eyes on me and saw in them a gleam of humour as he recognised the story I'd told him on the boat. But he concealed it from Grandad and asked in a suitably awed voice, 'You beat them off at the door?'

'Of course I did. There's nothing I wouldn't do for my little girl.'

Jack suddenly began to concentrate on his plate. I could see him restraining his laughter with difficulty, but Grandad, lost in lyrical flight, noticed nothing amiss.

He became expansive. The rest of the family crept into the conversation, with all the riper stories raked up and relived. I made feeble attempts to stop him, but somehow Jack always sabotaged these efforts, so at last I gave up and went with the flow.

Even so, I wasn't for prepared for Jack saying, 'We'll have them all to the party.'

'Party?' Grandad's eyes popped.

'The party to celebrate Della's return. We'll fix a date and you must call them all up.'

'Jack,' I said nervously, 'I don't think that's a very good idea—'

His eyes flashed, warning me to say no more. 'I think it's a great idea.'

''Course it is!' Grandad yelped. 'We'll have a great party. Leave it all to me.' He patted my hand. 'Just wait till they see this place, luv. It'll make their eyes pop.'

I groaned, and hid my head in my hands, but Jack seemed unfazed.

When the meal was over Grandad had an attack of tact and went off to bed. I think Jack and I were equally embarrassed. I washed up, ignoring his protests, and went to my own room.

Getting to sleep wasn't easy, and when I did

nod off I awoke after a couple of hours. I got up and went out, meaning to head for the kitchen. But the light from my room, falling onto the sofa, showed me the last thing I'd expected.

Jack was stretched out under a blanket. I stayed still for a moment, watching him, holding my breath. With his daytime patina of confidence gone, he looked worn and haggard. I'd thought he looked older at the prison, but this was worse.

I'd done this to him.

I crept closer and sat down on a stool where I could see his face more closely. The last time I'd seen him asleep had been on the boat, when we'd both been full of loving and his face had shown blissful contentment. Not any longer.

The noise of snoring had been coming faintly from beyond the bedroom door. Now it suddenly increased, causing Jack to give a start and wake up. He didn't show any surprise to find me there, but yawned and stretched.

'Hello,' he said sleepily.

'I'm sorry about this. Grandad driving you out, I mean. I guess you didn't know what you were taking on.'

He grinned ruefully.

'I admit the snoring takes some getting used to, but he's a great old boy.'

'Just the same, this can't go on. You need your sleep, and you don't need to have your days disrupted. I think Grandad and I should go home tomorrow.'

'Great, if you want to get me into real trouble.'

'What do you mean? I'm not going to abscond. I'll turn up in court on the right day.'

'You don't understand. I'm standing surety for you. The court needed a promise about where you'd stay, and the lawyer gave them this address. If you move out they'll haul *me* into court.'

I just gaped at him. I'd faced court in a haze, and I hadn't understood this.

'You promised them that I'd stay in your home?'

'I didn't say anything about it being mine. I still officially live with Grace. Nobody will connect me.'

'They will in the end. Jack, you're taking such risks for me.'

'You've taken a few risks yourself, haven't you?'

'But not for you. You don't owe me anything.'

'Yes I do. Selina married Derek. I guess that's down to you.'

'I saw it in the papers. Big society do. Has Grace tried to pair you off with anyone else?'

'No. I think she's understood now that my stubbornness is greater than her cunning.'

'You're not too bad in the cunning stakes yourself,' I observed wryly.

'Thanks to you. I'm in your debt.'

'Is that what you're doing now? Paying a debt you think you owe me?'

He shrugged. 'I guess. Why not? Paying debts in full and on time is good business practice.' He said the last words with slow emphasis.

'And you believe in good business practice?' I hazarded.

'It's what makes the world go round.'

'Isn't it supposed to be love that does that?'

'Supposed to be. But that's an old wives' tale. Business is more reliable. But you have to do it right. When I've finished we'll be even. All debts paid, loose ends tied up. And then,' he added in an almost inaudible voice, 'then maybe I can sleep.'

He was still stretched out on the sofa. I dropped down beside him and he took hold of my shoulders. He was looking straight up at me, but I had a strange feeling he couldn't see me.

'Sleep,' he whispered again. 'But then I'd

wake and hear you crying, like that last morning. I was never sure whether I imagined it or not.'

'You didn't imagine it,' I said. 'I was crying at leaving you.'

'I never stopped hearing that sound, night after night.' He closed his eyes tight, as if in pain. 'You shouldn't have left me with that in my ears.'

'I shouldn't have done anything the way I did,' I whispered. 'I got everything wrong. I thought I was doing the right thing. I didn't mean to hurt you, Jack. I thought I was just a holiday romance.'

'Was that what I was to you?'

'Oh, no, no!'

He stroked a wisp of hair away from my forehead. 'Why couldn't you have trusted me?' he said. 'When I found you'd gone I nearly went crazy. It was like coming to an oasis in the desert and then finding it was only a mirage. And then the desert is all around you and there's no way out.'

'You're asking me to use hindsight,' I pleaded. 'At the time it felt like the right thing to do. Maybe if I'd told you everything from the start it might have been different, but I felt as if I'd tricked you into loving me by hiding the truth.'

There was a silence before he said in an odd voice, 'Meaning that if I'd known the truth I wouldn't have loved you?'

'Meaning that you'd have been warned in time and you could have been cautious before it was too late.'

He stared at me for a moment, then rose so sharply that I slid to the floor.

'Thanks,' he said harshly. 'That's all I needed.'

'What?'

'That's what you think of me? Cold-blooded, calculating, willing and *able* to be cautious once I've assessed the conditions and found them unsuitable? You call that love? Damn you, that's an insult to everything I ever felt for you.'

'Jack, I didn't mean—'

'I know what you meant, and I call it arrogance. *You* made the decision for both of us. *You* thought you were the only one who could decide. Did it ever occur to you that I was a thinking human being who liked to make his own decisions? Maybe I could have coped. Maybe I could have found a way around it.'

I no longer tried to stop him. What was coming out was a stream of rage that had been building up for a long time.

'Della, did it ever occur to you that your

family of small-time con artists is no big deal? You think you're the only one who's got friends in jail? Last year I nearly did some business with a fellow whose company I really enjoyed. He was funny, bright, well-mannered, and an expert in his field. But the negotiations got nowhere because he was arrested for massive fraud. He's currently doing ten years in a New York jail for filching thirty million.'

That silenced me.

'There are probably more crimes committed in my world than yours,' Jack went on. 'Only they're mostly dressed up so that they don't look like crimes. Bribery, corruption—you name it. I don't go in for it myself, but I know people who do. I can't help that. It's a fact of life. So maybe your folks buy stuff that fell off the back of a lorry? Big deal!'

I'd picked myself up off the floor and sat down on the sofa again. He gave an exasperated sigh and sat down beside me.

'I know my way around the big jungle, Della. I can cope with it. And I could sure as hell have coped with your little jungle.'

I felt winded. Had I been arrogant? Denying him the right to make his own decisions? Had I thrown everything away for nothing?

And it had been totally thrown away, because I'd heard him speaking in the past tense. He'd said, *I could have coped*, not *I can cope*.

'I'm sorry,' I said. 'I never thought of it that way.'

His anger had passed, and he took my hand. It wasn't the start of anything, just a friend comforting a friend.

'How have you been?' he asked quietly.

'Sad,' I said. 'You?'

He nodded. After a while he said heavily, 'I found the jewellery where you said it was. There was no need for that. It was rightfully yours. I gave it to you.'

'I could never really feel it was mine,' I said. 'Except Charlie.'

He rose and went to a small chest of drawers, returning after a moment and holding something out to me. It was Charlie.

'Take him,' he said. 'He's always been yours.'

'Thank you.'

I took him gratefully. As everything else had been taken away I had clung to Charlie, sitting up at night and holding him in my hand like a talisman. Losing him had been like losing Jack again. Now the sight of him made me smile.

'I haven't seen you smile since we met again,' he said.

'I'm glad to have him back,' I said softly. 'I've missed him so much.'

'Only him?' he asked quietly.

'No, not only him. But he was really mine. I didn't think you could ever be.'

'That's not true, Della. I was all yours. But maybe we were never as close as I thought. Was I only fooling myself, then?'

'Perhaps you were. When I wouldn't tell you about myself, maybe you filled the blank spaces with a fantasy.'

'And are words all that count? When you came into my arms that last night, don't you think my heart knew you then in the only way that matters? Didn't your heart know me?'

I nodded, feeling a lump in my throat. 'Yes,' I said. 'It knew everything.'

I was crying as I said it, and he reached out and held me close. I put my arms about him and we sat there for a while, comforting each other and mourning what we'd had and lost.

CHAPTER ELEVEN

Della's Story

JUST as I'd feared, Jack insisted on having the party. Grandad began planning the food, but Jack managed tactfully to steer him away.

'I don't think beans on toast will quite meet the case,' he said.

'He can do other things.' I defended Grandad. 'Sardines on toast, cheese on toast, mushrooms on toast.'

'I think I'll stick to my catering firm.'

For a few days we didn't see him. He was spending his nights at the house he nominally shared with Grace. Grandad became sentimental.

'Knight in shining armour,' he declared. 'He won't stay here in case he compromises you.'

'Grandad, come into the twenty-first century,' I begged. 'Nobody thinks like that any more.'

'What else could it be?'

I could imagine another reason. The night

Jack and I had talked, we'd got closer than we'd meant to. Now I reckoned he was embarrassed to be with me in case I started hoping for more than he had to offer.

But I didn't say that to Grandad. I just murmured something about his snoring, he hotly denied that he ever snored, and we left it at that.

Jack returned unexpectedly one evening when Grandad had gone to bed. He looked harassed.

'Grace won't let the subject alone and it's doing my head in,' he groaned.

'The subject being me?'

'You, and my foolishness in getting mixed up…etc. etc.'

'Put your feet up. I'll make you some supper.'

'It's not beans on toast, is it?' he asked in alarm.

I laughed. 'No. Scrambled eggs, because they're nice and light.'

We sat down at the table together and he ate with relish.

'Grace laid on a fantastic meal tonight,' he said, 'and I could hardly eat any of it for the indigestion she was giving me.'

'Poor Grace,' I said.

He stared at me. 'That's the last thing I expected you to say.'

'Well, she sent you to my rescue, however
little she meant to. Maybe I owe her one. I
can't help seeing that she's scared and miser-
able. You're all she has. The days when you
really did need her were probably her happiest
ones and she's trying to keep some part of them
alive.'

'But why can't she see that she's doing it the
wrong way?'

'The really sad thing is that she probably
does see it,' I mused. 'Grace isn't a fool. She
must know that when she nags you she drives
you further away, but she doesn't know how to
do anything else. It gets her your attention,
even if you do storm out afterwards. But then
she knows that she's irritated you and she gets
more scared, and nags harder, and so it be-
comes a vicious circle.'

'So what do I do?'

'I don't know. But maybe if she felt that you
understood—'

'I can't be understanding when she starts
abusing you,' he said firmly.

'Then change the subject. Get her to talk
about something else, and be nice about that.'

He shook his head in a kind of wonder. 'If

Grace only knew that you were fighting her corner.'

'Don't tell her, for heaven's sake!' I begged. 'That would really upset her.'

He grinned. I poured him some more tea.

'How are the party arrangements going on?' he asked.

'Everyone in my family has accepted,' I said, in such a tense voice that he looked at me askance.

'You really disapprove, don't you?'

'I can't see why you're doing it. I'm just going to be embarrassed out of my mind.'

'Why?'

'Because I've heard Grandad on the phone to them. You can't imagine the stories he's telling.'

He gave me a wide grin.

'Nonsense. Of course I can imagine. I know him by now. He's so much like Grandpa Nick that it's weird.'

'But you don't know my family. The first thing they ask themselves is, ''Where's the profit?'''

'Very wise. I ask myself that every day.'

'But they'll be trying to profit from *you*. They'll look at you and see rich pickings. Jack, they'll try to fleece you.'

'Darl—Della, I spend my days with people

who are trying to fleece me. I can take care of myself. Stop treating me like an idiot.'

'All right,' I said crossly. 'I've tried to warn you but you won't be warned. And when one of them has sold you a non-existent gold mine you'll know I was right.'

'I can add it to my other non-existent gold mines. Anyway, you never know. I might sell them one.'

'I wish you'd be serious.'

'Now you're sounding like Grace. Does it occur to either of you that I've had enough of being serious? I'm ready to be something else. I'm just not quite sure what.'

He fell silent, and I had a feeling that he'd floated away from me. He was looking inside himself, or out at some far distant horizon. Or both at once. Certainly his voice had become dreamy in a way that didn't sound like his normal self.

'Well, at least when you've met them you'll know the worst,' I said.

'Della, when will you understand that I don't define you by your family? And you shouldn't define yourself that way either.'

'I don't.'

'You do, otherwise you wouldn't make such efforts to hide them. They are what they are, and you are what you are, and it's not the same. You're innocent.'

'I'm still facing a jail sentence,' I pointed out.

'Always assuming that it gets to court. The owners may be satisfied with having the bracelet back.'

'Why should they be? They haven't been so far. According to Mr Wendell they're dead keen for the police to prosecute. He found out that they had something stolen before and the thief got away. So now they've got hold of me they're not going to let go.'

'They might still change their minds and withdraw the charges.'

'Jack, it's a crime to nobble witnesses. You could end up behind bars yourself.'

'*Nobble witnesses?* What an extraordinary suggestion!'

'I'm sorry. I thought that was what you were talking about.'

'Not a bit of it. If I— That is, nobbling witnesses is very crude, and I prefer subtlety.' Then he changed the subject abruptly. 'What are you going to wear for the party?'

'I've still got one of those cocktail dresses you bought me. It's blue silk, very nice.'

'Only I was thinking—'

'I know, but there's no need, thank you.'

There was a touch of desperation in his voice, 'You won't take anything from me, will you?'

'How can you say that when I'm actually taking so much from you?'

He smiled, but it seemed forced. 'Yes, you're right. Let's leave it.'

On the day of the party he was home early, and noticed me at a loose end.

'What's wrong?'

'I've got nothing to do,' I complained.

'So I should hope. Leave it to the caterers.'

'Anyway, Grandad's happy.'

'They haven't let him touch anything, have they?' he asked, aghast.

'He's being allowed to cut cheese, that's all. As long as he's busy he's happy.'

'Della, how long can you go on subordinating everything to his needs?'

'I've told you—he deserves it.'

'Yes, sure. He looked after you and you're looking after him, but he didn't come forward to get you out of this mess, did he?'

'Because I told him not to.'

'The hell with that. Do you think *I'd* leave you to rot because you told me to?'

'Jack, it's not fair to criticise him. He's an old man—'

'I'm not criticising him. He's more than old, he's scared stiff, or he wouldn't have let it get this far. I don't blame him for being too scared to do the right thing, but who looks after you?'

I didn't answer.

'It's going to get worse, Della. It'll happen again, and what will you do next time?'

'I'll think about that when it happens,' I muttered.

'I'm thinking of it now. Will you wake up and look ahead? He's got the mind of a child. A loveable, crazy child, but the burden on you is going to get greater.'

'It's my burden and I'll cope,' I said crossly, remembering to add, 'But of course I appreciate what you're doing.'

He grinned at that hasty afterthought. To my relief he dropped the subject.

It was soon time to dress for the evening. I put on the blue dress, and when I'd pinned Charlie on the shoulder I looked quite presentable.

Jack didn't say anything when he saw me, but he smiled and nodded. He was smartly but casually dressed, and looked as handsome as I remembered from the boat. His appearance had improved and he no longer looked ill these days.

Then I noticed his cufflinks. They were the

shabby ones given him by Grandpa Nick. As though he was going to need good luck tonight.

He saw me looking at them, smiled self-consciously and pulled his jacket sleeves down to hide them.

'Jack—'

'They'll be here in a moment. Are we ready?'

So he left me not knowing what to think, which was how it normally was these days.

Nobody was late. They all wanted to get a look at Jack. I had a busy time introducing them to him and him to them.

They were a good-looking bunch, I realised. Harry, his wife and two sons; Alec, sporting a black eye, his wife and grown-up son and daughter; Hetta with her three daughters, all beauties. Bill had no family, but he was a natural clown with a gift for making the party go. David and Ken were the other brothers, with five offspring between them.

I'd expected to hate it, but almost at once I knew that the party had the magic ingredient that would make it gel. In part it was Jack, who romanced every female in sight, from Hetta's sultry daughter, Penny, to Lil, Alec's stern-faced wife.

She had a lot to look stern about. Alec was fond of her, but he was a philanderer, and I guessed the black eye meant he'd been straying again.

Jack took personal charge of Lil—keeping an eye on her drink, joking with her, and looking deep into her eyes in a way that made her blush. I could see that she was forgetting everyone around her. Jack could have that effect on people.

Alec could see it too, and he didn't like it. Leaving a group of men who were enjoying Jack's finest single malt whisky, he edged forward until he was standing beside her.

'Lil—'

She didn't seem to hear.

'Lil—' He touched her arm.

She looked at him as if she'd never seen him before.

Alec was staggered. He was used to having Lil's full attention, and to her letting him get away with anything because she loved him more than he loved her.

'What is it?' she asked.

'Er—why don't you come over here and talk to Bill?'

But Lil was enjoying the full blast of Jack's charm and she wasn't going to budge. I didn't blame her.

'I've known Bill for years,' she told her husband firmly. 'Why should I want to talk to him now?'

'Well—'

She turned back to Jack. 'Go on with what you were saying.'

Having received his dismissal, Alec drifted unhappily away.

There were other moments about that evening that I enjoyed very much. Ken, for instance, assuming that all businessmen were crooks of one kind or another, explaining to Jack in lurid detail exactly how he'd ripped off a firm called Callon Inc.

'Very ingenious,' Jack said, straight-faced. 'I never knew there were such flaws in the security system. I must have a talk with them first thing on Monday.'

'You?'

'I own that firm. Didn't I say?'

Ken blenched. 'No, you didn't say.'

'I'm grateful to you. You've done me a favour. Perhaps you'd care to look over some other firms of mine and tell me where they can be attacked.'

Ken looked suspicious. 'You mean—you're not going to cut up rough?'

'I'd look a bit silly doing it now, wouldn't I?'

Later Jack had a long chat with David. I

couldn't make out details, but from the way they had their heads together it seemed very man to man. I discovered afterwards that David—who, as everyone agreed, had never been the brightest tool in the box—had asked his advice on the best way to manage the extra activities with which he supplemented the income he earned from his 'antiques' shop.

Only when it was too late did he remember that Jack was on the other side of the fence, so to speak. I saw him gulp as realisation hit, and I saw Jack grin at him, then put his finger over his lips.

'You're a fraud,' I told him softly. 'You're making them think you're one of them.'

'Why shouldn't I be—in spirit, anyway? Della, tell me something. Do any of your family indulge in rough stuff—knocking people about, that sort of thing?'

'Certainly not,' I said, offended. 'They've *never* been like that.'

He nodded. 'That's what I thought. Hetta come and have a drink with me.'

By time there was music playing, and when they'd drunk champagne he swept her into the dance.

She was only allowed to keep him for one dance. All the pretty young girls were queuing up to be his partner, but he made them wait, asking the older women first.

I still wonder what alchemy made him invite Lil to dance to pop music. How did he know that hidden in that heavy body was the girl who'd wowed them at the disco twenty years ago? It took only a few brash chords to lure her out again, and then she and Jack were flinging themselves all over the place. Everyone cheered and clapped, and with the last chord Jack drew her back into a theatrical simulation of an embrace.

Alex didn't like that, I was happy to see. He didn't like it at all.

I remembered the dances on *The Hawk*, all the tension, the edginess, the attitudes, with nobody relaxed. Jack looked far more at home at this one, I had to admit.

Ken drifted by while Jack was dancing with Penny.

'You've landed on your feet,' he murmured to me.

Ken has always been crude.

'It's not like that,' I said.

'Go on. I know what these apartments cost. I investigated them last year for a client, and if Jack can afford this, then, like I say, you've landed on your feet.'

'I haven't landed anywhere. There's nothing between us.'

'So why's he giving you a party and meeting your family? I don't see any other guests here.'

I couldn't answer that.

'Well, if you don't want him there's plenty who do. Look at Penny, for instance.'

'I should think everyone's looking at Penny,' I said, trying not to sound as grouchy as I felt.

'Very nice-looking girl. She's recently been doing some glamour modelling. Big success. She's got a gift for it, if you know what I mean.'

I knew exactly what he meant.

Ken moved off and Grandad took his place, saying to me, 'Don't let them see you mind, luv.'

'I do not mind,' I said, a tad sharply.

'Then why are you looking as if you've swallowed a lemon?'

'I'm not.'

'You are.'

'Well, I'm a wallflower, aren't I?' I complained. 'Who can I dance with?'

'You can dance with me.'

'Right, I will.'

We took the floor together, but I didn't get to keep him long. Lil, still alight from her moment of glory, claimed him, and they kicked up their heels together. Alec didn't like that either, but there was nothing he could say without looking ridiculous, Grandad being so old.

I got one dance with Jack, at the end of the evening, but it was a very sedate affair. The feel of his hands through the dress's thin material, his warm breath on my shoulders, destroyed all my good resolutions to keep my distance.

Jack, on the other hand, seemed well able to resist the temptation to draw me close. It was almost worse than not dancing with him at all.

The evening ended in a riot of good cheer. Everyone but me seemed to know what it had all been about. They'd sized him up, he'd sized them up, they all knew where they stood with each other and seemed happy with the result.

Just one big happy family, in fact.

If there's one thing my folks know how to do, it's enjoy themselves. When they had gone, and the caterers had departed, the place looked as though a bomb had hit it.

Grandad and I did a bit of half-hearted tidying, but Jack said to leave the rest, because the cleaners would come in the morning.

He was on the sofa, leaning back, staring at the ceiling, a look of seraphic happiness on his face.

'Are you all right?' I asked him.

'Yes, thank you. It was a very satisfactory evening.'

'I guess it was. When you weren't being swarmed over by women I saw all the men sizing you up.'

'Uh-huh!' He laughed. 'But I don't think they'll do it again.'

I began to get the picture. Or at least some of it.

'I saw you talking to Harry,' I mused.

'Which one was Harry?'

'The respectable one—the lawyer.'

'Ah, yes! Oddly enough, he's the only one who actually looks like a crook. He kept telling me that his firm was looking to branch out into corporate law, providing a top-quality service for a very select clientele.'

'Jack, no! Even Harry doesn't suffer from that much self-delusion.'

'Now, there you're wrong. There is no limit to his self-delusion. He was the only one I disliked. The others are all honest rogues.' He laughed suddenly. 'Why was Alec sporting a black eye? Gang warfare?'

'Only the kind that goes on in his home every day. Lil caught him grazing in forbidden pastures. She tends to get physical when she's provoked. Come to think of it, she was getting very physical with you on the dance floor.'

'She's a good dancer, but I don't think she's had much chance recently. I'm sure Alex doesn't take her out.'

'I think he might now,' I said, chuckling.

'Who's the one with jet black hair?'

'David's wife, Angie.'

'She lectured me about how all men need keeping in their place. She says she's tried to pass her theories on to you.'

He regarded me quizzically, but I refused to be drawn.

'I don't take second-hand theories,' I said loftily. 'I prefer to invent my own.'

A smile came into his eyes. 'That's my girl. Ah, well, I'm sorry it's over. I really enjoyed it.'

'Yes, I saw you enjoying it with Penny,' I said coolly. 'She was the one in the see-through dress, in case you didn't catch the name. I hope you got a good look at everything.'

'If I didn't it's no fault of hers. Hetta wants me to back her in a modelling career. Or becoming a pop star. I don't think it matters as long as I come across with the necessary.'

'Are you going to?'

'Not a chance. I've brought saying 'Uh-huh!' in a non-committal voice to a fine art. Mind you, I've had years of practice with Grace.' He gave a wry smile. 'It was fun. I'd forgotten about fun.'

His eyes were shining. I smiled back, loving to see him like that.

'Goodnight, Jack,' I said.

'Goodnight, Della.'

He rose from the sofa and half turned away, then swung around and grasped hold of me without warning, pulled me against him and kissed me hard.

His arms were very tight around me, so that I couldn't clasp him back even if I'd been able to think clearly. I had nothing to do but stand there and be kissed, very thoroughly.

Now I knew how much I'd wanted to be kissed. His lips felt so good on mine. I'd missed him so much.

Then, as suddenly as it had begun, it was over.

'Goodnight,' he said breathlessly, and vanished.

I stood there for a while, trying to calm my nerves, wondering what was happening to me.

CHAPTER TWELVE

Jack's Story

I USED a private detective to find out all about Bentley Cunningham, the man whose wife had lost the diamond bracelet.

'He's like a bit of theatre scenery,' the detective told me after he'd rooted around a bit. 'Looks good from the front but it's all one-dimensional, there's nothing behind. A breath of the wrong financial wind could blow him flat. He inherited his company from his father and he's let most of it slip through his fingers. His wife has no idea. She still thinks he's a big success, so he has to keep up the pretence. That bracelet was a way of fooling her, but he had to take out an expensive loan to buy it. And it wasn't insured, so they got very upset when they thought it had gone for good.'

His company made machine tools and was situated near the Thames. As soon as I approached it I could see the signs that said he needed a friendly investor badly.

When I introduced myself I was glad to see he knew my name. That would make it a lot easier.

What wasn't easy was actually doing what I intended. It had been simple to plan it inside my head, but this was reality, where I had to get it right first time, and I was nervous.

That's right. Bully Jack was going to do a bit of manipulating, and he was nervous because it mattered more than anything had mattered in his life.

I'd spent sleepless nights thinking of my darling going back to jail. In the early hours I'd made idiotic plans. I would take her and Grandad and we would vanish, spending the rest of our lives on a barge, cruising the waterways. They would look for us in vain.

Anything was better than seeing her suffer for even a few minutes, let alone a few months.

Approaching Cunningham meant violating every principle I had. But I was discovering what principles were really for. They were for ditching when you found out what mattered most to you. Della mattered more than anything or anyone, and to hell with principles.

So, for the first time ever, I indulged in the kind of behaviour for which Bully Jack was already famous.

Not that there was any bullying needed. Poor

Cunningham was a decent little man who was out of his depth. When he heard my proposal he thought Christmas had come. I ended up poorer, he ended up richer and beaming with relief. And Della ended up safe.

As soon as I was out of there I called Wendell.

'I want you to handle this investment as well as looking after Della,' I said. 'Then you can see that they're properly co-ordinated.'

He agreed to call Cunningham at once, then the police.

As I returned to the flat I pictured Della's face when she heard the news, but it was strangely difficult. Her relief was easy to imagine. It was the bit afterwards that caused me trouble. How would she be? Awkward? Embarrassed? Even a little hostile? I could imagine anything these days. I didn't really know who she was.

It made no difference. Whoever she turned out to be, she'd got under my skin and into my heart, and she was there for life. But I didn't know what she felt about anything, especially me. She'd been very quick to assure me that she had no 'illusions' about our love reviving. But was that her way of putting me at ease? Or of saying it was really over? I was about to find out.

I entered the apartment full of anticipation and trepidation in equal measure, but it was an anticlimax. Only Grandad was there.

'What have you been up to?' he asked as soon as he saw my face. I was still partly in a state of shock.

'Bribery and corruption,' I said slowly.

'Good for you,' he said at once. 'Any use?'

'Oh, yes. The charges are going to be dropped.'

He gave a yelp of glee and began to dance around like a little kid, carolling tunelessly.

'Where is she?' I asked.

'Doing a bit of shopping. But she only just went, so she might be a couple of hours.'

The thought of waiting there for two hours suddenly made my stomach churn. I needed to be doing something as the most important moment of my life drew near.

'I have to go,' I said. 'I'll be back later. Bye Nick.'

'What did you call me?'

'Er—Grandad. See ya!'

I went to my office, to be met by the news that Grace was waiting for me.

I found her sitting in a chair by the window I saw her before she saw me, and caught a look of misery on her face that she normally hid. As soon as she glanced up the old look was back

It was armoured and guarded for war, but I wasn't fooled now. I was remembering what Della had told me about her.

'I came because it seems the only way to see you,' she said curtly. 'You're never home and you're always busy.'

'I'm not too busy for you,' I said, sitting beside her. 'I'm glad you're here, because I've got a lot to tell you.'

'I can imagine. I heard about your party for your low-life friends. I'm not surprised I was excluded from that. All you think about now is how to make life easy for your little crook.'

'She's not a crook. The charges have been dropped.'

'I suppose you did that?'

'Yes, I did it.'

'May I ask how?'

'They were dropped because she's innocent. She always was.'

She didn't answer and I took her hands. 'Gracie, come on—'

She tried to snatch her hands away. 'Don't call me Gracie.'

I kept hold. 'I'll call you Gracie if I want to. It's what I used to call you, remember? When I was a boy?'

'That was a long time ago.'

'Not that long. You called me Jacko and I called you Gracie. We were happy then.'

I could see that the memory had softened her a little, but she wasn't going to give in too easily.

'We're not those people any more.'

'Yes, we are,' I insisted. 'That was our past. Ours. Yours and mine. And nobody else can ever share it or know about it.'

She looked at me.

'Not even Della?'

'Not even Della,' I said, knowing I had to conceal how much Della had contributed to this moment. 'You were a second mother to me, and nobody else knows what that means. I miss it, Gracie. I miss how close we were. Don't you?'

'Yes,' she whispered, holding onto my hands now. 'But you grew up and went away.'

'You used to say I'd never grow up, and you were right. I'm still Jacko inside, and I always will be. Only to you, of course. I wouldn't let anyone else call me that.'

She smiled hesitantly. 'Jacko,' she said.

I drew her to her feet.

'Come on, I'm taking you to lunch. Things are happening, and I want you to be the first to know about them.'

I told my secretary to hold all calls, and we

went out to the Ritz. It was a long lunch, and a happy one. It was years since we had felt so close. I told her all about my future plans, and although I could see she was shocked she didn't make an issue of it. Near the end of lunch I slipped out to call Harry Oxton.

Grace didn't seem surprised when he turned up to escort her home. She gave me a smile I hadn't seen for years and said significantly, 'I see Jacko the Joker is still alive.'

'Good grief!' I exclaimed. 'That was one of your names for me too.'

'Or sometimes Jumping Jacko.'

'Yes, I remember now. Those names were truer than Bully Jack ever was, and I think they'll be happier than he ever was.'

'That all depends on her answer, I suppose?' Grace said.

'Yes, and it's far from certain. Cross your fingers for me, Gracie.'

'I will. The very best of luck—Jacko.'

We hugged each other tightly, and she went off with Harry.

Now I had the real mountain to climb. I ought to go round there, but I found myself putting it off. There was no hurry. She would know she was safe by now, and that was what mattered.

The truth was that I was scared to face her.

Della's story

Grandad pounced on me as soon as I got home.

'You're in the clear,' he carolled. 'They're dropping the charges.'

'Where did you hear that?'

'Jack told me. He was here. He went to see Cunningham and got him to agree.'

'But how did he do that?'

'Bribery and corruption, he said. Oops!' He put his hand to his mouth. 'He made me promise not to tell you.'

I hardly heard. I was beginning to realise that Jack hadn't stayed around to tell me the good news himself.

'Where is he?' I asked.

'He said he had to go.'

'Did he say when he'd be back?'

Grandad shrugged.

Mixed with relief there was a sinking feeling inside me. Jack had done what he promised, but it hadn't mattered enough to him to tell me himself and see my face. He couldn't have told me more clearly that I was in the past.

All that day I was sure he'd call me, but the phone stayed silent. Didn't he even want to hear about my joy? Didn't he want to bother with me at all?

At last I gave in and called his office.

'I'm sorry,' his secretary told me. 'Mr Bullen said to hold all calls.'

I hung up and sat staring at the phone.

It rang and I seized it up. 'Jack?'

'No, it's Thomas Wendell. Just to keep you up to date with what's happening. The police have confirmed to me that the case has been dropped, seeing as the Cunninghams have withdrawn the charges.'

'Because of Mr Bullen?'

'Oh, yes. He's been pulling strings like crazy. He's investing a fortune in that clapped-out firm, and I don't think he'll see much of it back. You'll be getting written confirmation, but you can take it as definite. It's all over.'

I thanked him politely but I was in a daze. His last words stood out in neon.

It's all over.

Of course he'd been talking about the case, but there was an ominous second meaning.

It's all over.

And it was. All over. Jack had done what he'd promised. He'd cleared whatever he'd thought was on his conscience and now he could forget me. In fact he'd started to forget me already.

'When Jack comes back we'll have a special celebration meal,' Grandad said. 'Beans on toast.'

'He's not coming, Grandad, and we should start packing.'

'Packing? What are you talking about, luv?'

'He's helped us out and that's it. I'm an embarrassment to him.'

'You mean we're an embarrassment.' He looked crestfallen. 'Is that why he keeps getting my name wrong?'

I didn't answer. I was too preoccupied to hear this properly, or consider the implications.

It suddenly seemed terrible to be here, where we had no right to be, and I couldn't wait to get out.

I had to write to him, and for some reason this letter was harder than the other one. I told him how grateful I was, thanked him, and promised to be no further trouble to him.

When I read it over I was thoroughly dissatisfied with it, but I knew I couldn't do any better.

We packed up quickly and went out into the street. A few minutes' walk brought us to the nearest tube station, and an hour later we were entering our own little home.

Grandad went to bed early. I sat up late, waiting for the phone to ring. Of course it didn't. It was early light when I went upstairs and fell into a doze. It lasted on and off until the dawn, when I was awoken by the sound of someone banging on the front door.

I threw the window open and yelled, 'Oi, I don't know what you—?'

I stopped at the sight of Jack's furious face glaring up at me.

'Della, you have two seconds to get yourself down here and let me in. Then I'm breaking the door down.'

I was still pulling on my dressing gown as I opened the front door. He was inside in a moment, still furious.

'A nice way to behave!' he snapped. 'You couldn't wait around to see me, could you? Once it was settled you couldn't get out fast enough. Well, that tells me where I stand.'

'Jack, what—?'

'I love you—do you understand that? I'm mad about you. I wanted to make everything right for you, and kiss you, and tell you I'd love you for ever. And, not for the first time, you weren't there.'

'I wasn't there because you didn't want me,' I said indignantly. 'You left a message with Grandad, then you walked out and told your secretary not to take my calls. What was I supposed to think?'

He groaned and tore his hair. Now I was getting my second wind I could see that he needed a shave and looked exhausted.

'I didn't tell my secretary to refuse your calls,' he growled. 'I told her to hold everything.'

'Yes, because you didn't want to talk to me.'

He drew a long, exasperated breath and spoke as though restraining himself with difficulty.

'Now, look, Della, don't you try to act like the aggrieved party. This is the second time you've walked out on me, and enough is enough. Do you know what it felt like for me, going back to the apartment and finding that little note? It felt like the first time, only a hundred times worse. How could you do that to me again?'

'I'm sorry—I didn't think of it that way.'

'That's it! No more creeping out when I'm not there. This time you face me and say straight out that you don't love me. Tell me to my face to go to blazes. That would at least be honest.'

'How dare you say I don't love you?' I yelled. 'Why do you think everything happened this way?'

'I don't know why!' he yelled back. 'I don't know anything about you because you won't let me. Even now, when I've met your family, you're still keeping yourself hidden in the ways that matter. If you want to hide from me for ever, at least say so.'

'I don't want to hide from you.'

'Then what are you doing here?'

'I—I thought— I don't know what I'm doing here. It seemed right at the time.'

'And now?' He was looking at me intently.

'Now I'm confused about everything. Why didn't you tell me about Mr Cunningham yourself?'

'I lost my nerve. Della, why are you looking at me like that?'

I suppose I was looking strange, because belatedly something had just dawned on me.

'You said you loved me?' I said.

'Yes, I did. Several minutes ago. It took time for that to register.'

He spoke grumpily but he wasn't angry any more. Nor was I.

'Haven't you got anything to tell me?' he asked.

'I thought you were embarrassed. I thought—'

'No, no.' He stopped me with a finger over my lips. 'Those aren't the right words.'

'What are the right words?'

'You know them.'

I smiled at him. Inside I was smiling all over. 'I love you, Jack.'

He gave a yell of triumph. *'Those are the right words!'*

I don't know if he grabbed me or I grabbed him, but for a long time nobody said any words at all. And when we came up for air Grandad was in the kitchen, making tea.

'You two took your time,' he said as he poured for us. 'Is it on now? Or are you just waiting for something else to misunderstand each other about?'

'It's all on now,' Jack said, watching me with a warmth in his eyes that seemed to reach out and enfold me. 'It's on for life. Isn't it?'

I nodded. 'For life.'

'I wanted to tell you everything myself.'

'Including the bribery and corruption?'

'I guess I'm just one of the family. But I don't mean to make a career of it. It was just the once, for you. And I only left a message so that you should know as soon as possible. When I got back to the office I found Gracie there. So I took her to lunch and made everything right between us—the way you said.'

'*I* said?'

'You gave me the clue about how lonely she was. I followed that up, and you were right. I

made it easy to tell her that I'm leaving the firm
for a while.'

'What? But it's your firm. How can you
leave it?'

'I'll become a sleeping partner. Peter can run
things. Maybe in a couple of years I'll go back,
but I have other things I want to do first—if
you agree.'

'Tell me about the other things,' I said, but
I thought I knew the answer.

Grandad refilled his cup and Jack said ab-
sently, 'Thanks, Nick.'

'Why do you keep calling me Nick? Who's
Nick?'

Jack gave the grin I loved. 'I'll tell you that
when we're on our way.'

'Are we going somewhere?' Grandad asked.

'As soon as you're ready.'

He was like a big kid, keeping a secret. I
might guess the secret, but he was only going
to tell in his own good time—although I could
tell he was bursting with it.

The sun had started to come up when we left
the house, and Jack headed the car north, towards the nearby canal.

'So who's Nick?' Grandad demanded from
the back seat.

'He was my grandpa,' Jack told him. 'You're
so like him that it's eerie.'

Grandad considered. 'You mean he was an old fool too?'

Jack laughed. 'Something like that. But he was my old fool and I was nuts about him.'

We parked near a bridge and went to look down into the water.

'There,' Jack said. 'Do you see her? She's called *The Bluebell*.'

She was the loveliest barge I'd ever seen— a real, traditional canal boat, painted in bright colours. It spoke of long, lazy summer days drifting along dreamy waterways.

'A hobo of the canals,' I said. 'What about the dogs? Three of them, you said.'

'We'll have them too. Great, daft creatures lolling around, wanting to be petted all the time.'

'It sounds perfect,' I said happily.

'I should have done this years ago. But it never became really important until now.'

'Is she yours?'

'Not yet. Not until you've approved her. But I've got the key.'

We went below and looked around. She was more spacious than she looked from the outside, but she was also cosy.

'This can be Grandad's room,' Jack said, indicating a door.

'Then he's coming with us?' I asked eagerly

'I know better than to try to part you two. You wouldn't leave him behind, and if you did you'd never have a moment's peace, wondering what trouble he was getting himself into.'

I flung my arms around him.

'Can it really come true?' I asked.

'It's going to come true. We're going to make it—if it's what you really want?'

'It's what I want more than anything. But won't you miss your work?'

'Maybe in a few years,' he said. 'But not for ages. I have another life to live first—our life together. A different world, well away from the other one. I don't want to have to think of anything but you.'

'No Bully Jack?'

'Bully Jack only ever existed for a few moments, when he needed to do a bit of manipulating for you. Now he's gone for ever. All that's left is the man who loves you—'

'And whom I love.'

'It is true that you love me?' he asked with sudden urgency. 'I need to believe in that, because it's who I am. I have this strange feeling that if you don't love me I don't really exist.'

There were no words that would have convinced him, so I laid my lips on his and we stayed there for a long time.

'You have to exist,' I said. 'Because if you

don't, neither do I. And without you I never will. Just as before you there was nothing.'

'For me too,' he said softly. 'Nothing at all. But now, for the rest of our lives, we'll have everything.'

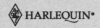
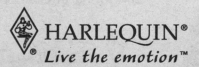

Harlequin Historicals®
Historical Romantic Adventure!

From rugged lawmen and valiant knights to defiant heiresses and spirited frontierswomen, Harlequin Historicals will capture your imagination with their dramatic scope, passion and adventure.

Harlequin Historicals . . . they're too good to miss!

HARLEQUIN®
INTRIGUE®

WE'LL LEAVE YOU BREATHLESS!

If you've been looking for thrilling tales of
contemporary passion and sensuous love stories
with taut, edge-of-the-seat suspense—then
you'll love Harlequin Intrigue!

Every month, you'll meet six new heroes
who are guaranteed to make your spine tingle
and your pulse pound. With them you'll enter
into the exciting world of Harlequin Intrigue—
where your life is on the line
and so is your heart!

THAT'S INTRIGUE—
ROMANTIC SUSPENSE
AT ITS BEST!

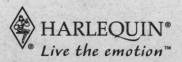

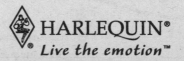